Dear Friend,

A couple of years ago, I started a novel about the writing life. As envisioned, the book would consist of an exchange of e-mails between two characters: a young, ambitious, aspiring writer and an old, published author. But as the book progressed, the day-to-day life of the young writer became so captivating that I could not help but tell his story.

One Last Chance to Live is the story of Nico Kardos told through his daily journal entries over a period of two months. Nico, a high school senior living in Hunts Point, the Bronx, has an ominous dream that his life will end the following summer. With a sense of urgency, Nico sets out to "become a great writer" by writing a publishable memoir. His ambition for fame and glory, however, is soon overtaken by the need to discover the circumstances surrounding the mysterious death of Rosario Zamora, the only girl he's ever loved.

With each day, Nico's journal becomes more and more the place where he confronts the suffering and oppression in his world as well as his own flaws and failures. Nico's initial motive to garner honor and admiration through writing gives way to an understanding that what matters most is responding with love to the people in his life.

This eleventh novel of mine is the most personal of all my books. Just as writing helped Nico find purpose and meaning in his dark days, so, too, have I found in my journal and my novels a way to give all I can to our hurting world. *One Last Chance to Live* is a gift from the heart, my gift to you, written with honesty.

Thank you for your friendship for this book, and for supporting my work through the years.

Francisco X. Stork

Title: One Last Chance to Live

Author: Francisco X. Stork

On-Sale Date: September 3, 2024

Format: Jacketed Hardcover

ISBN: 978-1-339-01023-6 || Price: $19.99 US

Ages: 12 and up

Grades: 7 and up

LOC Number: Available

Length: 320 pages

Trim: 5-1/2 x 8-1/4 inches

Classification: Young Adult:

Social Themes / Death, Grief, Bereavement / People &
Places / United States / Hispanic & Latino

Romance / Contemporary

Health & Daily Living / Diseases, Illnesses & Injuries

---------------- *Additional Formats Available* --------------
Ebook ISBN: 978-1-546-10966-2
Digital Audiobook ISBN: 978-1-5461-3693-4 || Price: $24.99 US
Library Audiobook ISBN: 978-1-5461-3694-1 || Price: $74.99 US

Scholastic Press
An Imprint of Scholastic Inc.
557 Broadway, New York, NY 10012
For information, contact us at:
tradepublicity@scholastic.com

ONE LAST CHANCE TO LIVE

FRANCISCO X. STORK

ONE LAST CHANCE TO LIVE

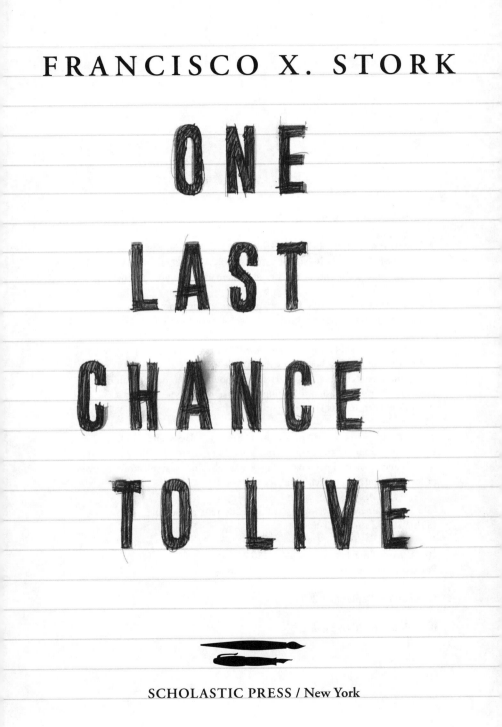

SCHOLASTIC PRESS / New York

Library of Congress Cataloging-in-Publication Data available
ISBN 978-1-339-01023-6

10 9 8 7 6 5 4 3 2 1   24 25 26 27 28
Printed in the U.S.A.   128

First edition, September 2024

Book design by Abby Dening

FOR MELISSA WETRICH STORK AND ALBERT
WILLEM KLOOSTERBOER

Mr. Cortazar—AP English

Journal of Nico Kardos
Monday, January 30

There are two creative writing classes at Stonebridge Charter. One is taught by the lovely Miss Falco and the other one by old man Cortazar. Even though Mr. Cortazar has a published novel under his name, most everyone chooses Miss Falco. This year there were only two students who signed up for Mr. Cortazar's class: me and Ruth Silvester, the shoo-in for valedictorian in a couple of months. Thirty other juniors and seniors signed up to take Miss Falco's class. To make things even, Mr. Rollo, our principal, put their names in a bowl and the first fifteen went to Miss Falco and the rest to Mr. Cortazar.

If you're a guy, watching Miss Falco for fifty minutes a day three times a week is a no-brainer unless you aspire to be a great writer, like me. But why, if you're a girl, would you still prefer someone who has trouble speaking correct English over an accomplished writer? According to Alma, who "got stuck" with Mr. Cortazar this semester, the reason everyone avoids Mr. Cortazar's class is the insane requirement to write a journal entry of at least five hundred words every single day, including Sundays. Seven thousand words sent to him electronically every two weeks.

Mr. Cortazar made a solemn promise during our first class that he will never read what we write in our journal. He will look at the word count and that's it. "You can copy the *Hunts Point Express* and I wouldn't know it," he told us. "You need to be absolutely certain no one will read what you write for a journal to work its magic on you."

Today, as we walked home, I told Alma what Mr. Cortazar said about never reading our journals and she smiled at me the way she does when she thinks I'm being naive.

"What, you think he's lying?" I asked.

"Mm-hmm."

"Can you tell me why you're so sure?"

"I could, but I won't."

I waited for a follow-up, but Alma started scrolling through her phone.

"Come on! You can't just say something like that." It was just like Alma to lead me to the top of the suspense cliff and leave me hanging.

Alma ignored me. The smile on her face told me she was responding to a text from Ruben. It was another ten minutes before she recognized my existence again. "What?"

"Why is Cortazar lying—about not reading our journals."

"Rosario . . ." Alma started to say, and then stopped. It was almost as if she had momentarily forgotten she didn't like talking about her older sister.

I, of course, would love nothing more than to talk about Rosario. "Rosario found out Mr. Cortazar read her journal?"

Alma stopped in the middle of the sidewalk and turned to me. "She wrote something in her journal and Cortazar brought it up . . . when she met with him. Okay?"

"Wait? What did Rosario write about? What happened when Rosario went to Mr. Cortazar's office?"

"I don't know. Probably something serious because when I asked her, she refused to talk about it." Alma began to walk at a fast clip. Over many years of walking home from school with Alma, I knew she sped up when she didn't want to answer whatever question I was about to ask.

I caught up with her. I knew Alma didn't like talking about Rosario, but this was important. "What do you mean by something serious must have happened? Did Rosario tell Mr. Cortazar something about how she was feeling or what was happening to her?"

"I'm telling you I don't know."

"But what do you think? What would Rosario and Mr. Cortazar talk about? Did Mr. Cortazar put a move on her? What? Why do you keep looking at me as if I'm stupid?"

"Ahh . . . maybe . . ."

I grabbed her arm and pulled her back onto the curb. A big white truck honked. "I may be stupid, but at least I don't get run over by fish trucks."

We waited for the walk sign and then crossed Hunts Point Avenue slowly. Alma's brown skin was a couple of shades paler. When we were on the other side, she said, a solemn tone in her voice, "I don't know for sure what they talked about, honestly."

"But you have a theory. I know you do."

There was loud hip-hop music coming from an appliances

4

store. Alma looked up at the speakers, and if she could have destroyed them with her sight, she would have. "Maybe . . . it was toward the end of the semester. She could have written something that raised an alarm. You know, teachers are supposed to recognize signs of depression, etcetera."

"But, I mean, what exactly did Rosario say to you?"

"She was supposed to take care of Pepito and she was late, as usual. I asked her where she'd been and she said Cortazar wanted to talk to her about something in her journal. That's all I know, okay? You happy? No more talk about Rosario." Alma shook her head angrily and ran the last block to our building, her red backpack and brown hair bouncing on her back.

I let her go and ducked into Osorio's bodega to buy a caffeinated energy drink in hopes it would stimulate my brain enough to understand what the hell had just happened. I walked over to the so-called playground behind our building. A group of X-Tecas smoking dope by the chain-link fence shouted their usual nasty remarks. I made sure my little brother, Javier, wasn't hanging out with them and then sat on one of the chipped cement benches.

I don't know why it took me so long to understand the full meaning of what Alma was saying. What Rosario wanted most of all was to be a great writer. That's what I want as well. By the end of her senior year, she had a book of short stories written already. Then a week after graduation, Rosario abruptly and mysteriously broke up with Noah, and a month later she was found dead from a heroin overdose in a hotel room in Queens. What happened? No one saw the end coming. Unless . . . maybe you saw something in her journal, Mr. Cortazar. If you're reading this, please tell me what you know about Rosario's last days of life . . . and death.

Tuesday, January 31, 2:30 a.m.

I want to quickly write down the dream that just happened. I was in a closed casket inside that dark, perfumy parlor in Ortiz's Funeral Home. Then I was floating on the ceiling watching the scene. I was surprised and disappointed that the small room was not even half-full. I'd been to funerals for dead kids where crowds spilled over onto the street.

In the front row sat Alma and her mother together with Noah. Behind them was my father sitting uncomfortably next to Harrison, my mother's boyfriend. Mr. Cortazar was there next to our school librarian, Mrs. Longoria, and next to them sat Ruth from my school, wearing a silky black dress and a necklace of tiny white pearls with matching earrings.

The rest of the rows were sparsely occupied with kids from school and people from the fish market.

The casket was the same one Mr. Ortiz used for Rosario. The same casket he always uses when the bodies are destined for incineration. Who can afford to be buried? No one I know and none of the families of the dozen dead kids who've used the casket. Sometimes the casket is open, like for Rosario's funeral, and sometimes it's closed, like when a gang member is shot in the face. In front of the casket was a red velvet kneeler and next to that a blown-up image of my yearbook picture. I hated that picture. It was taken the day after my wisdom teeth were pulled out, and I look like I'm chewing a huge wad of gum.

I searched to see if anyone was crying, but everyone seemed calm and even a little bored. The only evidence of grief I could find was Alma blowing her nose with a pink tissue, Noah's red eyes, and Ruth's lowered head. Then I noticed for the first time two empty chairs to the right of the casket. In the funerals I've attended, empty chairs were placed for the parents or siblings of the deceased that have previously departed from this world. Filled with sudden terror, I began looking for my mother and Javier. They weren't there. The two chairs were for them. Then things got dark, and I realized I was inside the coffin. I was unbearably sad because the two empty chairs on the front row meant my mother and Javier had already died. That's when I felt someone lying next to me in the coffin. I smelled coconut shampoo and knew it was Rosario. She was there to console me. For the loss of my mother and Javier. For my own death. For hers. I wanted to embrace her, but I couldn't turn. The coffin was too tight for two bodies. Rosario rose above me. Her whole being was made of a rose-colored light that was now dimming. She moved her hand in such a way that I could not tell whether she was asking me to follow her or waving goodbye. Then, just before she disappeared, she said something to me that I understood in the dream but could not remember when I woke up.

What, Rosario? What did you say to me?

Tuesday, January 31, 11:00 p.m.

After I finished writing down my dream this morning, I checked in on Javier and Julia (I call my mother by her first name) to make sure they were alive. Then I headed out to my job at the fish market, walking slowly, replaying in my mind all I could remember about my dream. I remembered that there were no coats draped over the backs of the chairs so it must have been summer. Did that mean I had a few months left of life? I remembered the sadness at the sight of those two empty chairs and how Rosario's presence comforted me. But most of all I thought about Rosario's wordless message. How could I have heard it so clearly in the dream and not know what she said upon awakening? What she spoke wasn't long or complicated. A few words at most. A simple statement, a request, maybe a question.

At one point during the day, I decided to share my dream with Alma. If only I could figure out a way of talking about Rosario without hurting her or stirring up painful memories. It was possible that Alma was mad at me. She seemed mad at me, for some reason, when we'd last spoken—that conversation about Rosario and Mr. Cortazar. This was not the first time I was clueless about what I had done to piss her off. Usually, she stopped talking to me after I lectured her about how incredibly irrational it was for her to be going out with Ruben. That conversation started with me saying something like "Do you know what he does for a living?" When the communication went well, it ended with Alma telling me to go to hell, and when it went bad, it ended with Alma silently sobbing.

I still remember the evening when I walked into Alma's apartment and, boom, there was Ruben sitting on the sofa holding hands with her. The following morning around five a.m., I was pacing the hall waiting to see a light come on from under Alma's door. When it did, I knocked, and her mom opened the door.

"Hey, Nico," Mrs. Zamora said, handing me Pepito. Pepito

11

is almost four years old and by no means underfed. "Can you give Pepe some cereal? I gotta get ready for work. My shift starts at seven now. They changed it from nine last week, the bastards, and it's killing me."

"Where's Alma?"

"Still sleeping. I don't even know what time she got in."

The Zamoras' apartment was an exact replica of ours, only on the opposite side of the hall. Three bedrooms, one bathroom, and a space that was combination kitchen, dining room, and living room. Mrs. Zamora disappeared into the bathroom. I plopped Pepito onto a chair by the kitchen table, gave him a bowl of cereal with lots of marshmallows, and then found the cartoon channel on the big-screen TV. I headed down the hall and knocked on the purple door to Alma's room. The purple door had been Rosario's idea when that was her room.

"Go away!" The voice was both hoarse and irritable—the sure signs of a medium-to-severe hangover.

I went in, pulled out the desk chair, and sat facing her. She opened half an eye and buried her head under a pillow.

"You cannot be serious," I said.

"Please go away. Not right now. Please!"

"Do you know what kind of business Ruben's in? Do you know what the X-Tecas must do to keep their business going? You may know *generally* who Ruben is and what he does, but do you know *specifically*? I will tell you because I work for those guys. Yeah, I sell weed for them at the fish market. I'm not proud to do it, but the extra cash helps, you know? Alma, I mean, are you nuts? Do you know half the people in his gang have been in prison or juvie? Primo spent ten years in prison for killing someone. And Ruben takes orders from this guy.

"Tell me it was a one-time thing. You got tired of being brilliant and you decided to be dumb and normal like the rest of us, just once, to get it out of your system. Was that it?"

"No." It was a muffled but definite no.

"No?"

Alma lifted the pillow and turned her face toward me with a snarl. "He asked me to be his girl and I said yes. He likes me and I like him. He's trying to get out of that life. He will. I believe him."

"You kidding, right? Ruben's the brains of X-Tecas. He handles all their finances. No way Primo lets him get out. The only way out for Ruben is in a body bag."

13

Alma covered her face with the pillow. I sat there, paralyzed, I don't know for how long, my hands gripping the edge of the chair, waiting for the sobs to stop. When they did and when I saw that she was breathing in a quiet rhythm, I walked out.

I told Mrs. Zamora through the closed bathroom door that I was taking Pepito to McDonald's and then to the playground so Alma could sleep a little longer.

"You're a sweetheart," Mrs. Zamora shouted. "Will you bring me a sausage biscuit? I'll eat it when I get home this afternoon."

Talking to Alma about Rosario is even more difficult than pointing out how Ruben is so wrong for her. Me talking about Rosario is like rubbing a raw wound and I was not up for a possible explosive response. I decided to hold off on telling Alma about my Rosario dream just then. As the day wore on, the dream's reality seeped into my blood, became part of me, and began to beat with every tick of my heart. It was good that most of that day's fish had been sold by the time I got to the fish market because for sure my mind was not on the job. All that was left for me to do was to throw away the used ice and wipe the aluminum bins that hold the fish—things I can do without thinking. The only mishap was accidentally lock-ing Noah in the stand-up freezer.

"What's up with you today?" Noah asked when I let him out. "You walkin' around half dead."

If he only knew.

Wednesday, February 1

I had an appointment with Mr. Cortazar this afternoon. Mr. Cortazar meets individually with the students in his writing class twice during the semester. All day long I wondered whether I would have the guts to ask him about Rosario, about reading Rosario's journal, about what he knew of her final days. I was so nervous on the way to his office, I had to make a long stop at the men's. Nerves affect my stomach something awful.

"How's the journal writing going? Are you keeping up with it?" Mr. Cortazar conducts the writing interviews in the same classroom where he teaches. The only difference from class is that he sits in a student's desk facing you.

"I wanted to talk to you about that. I'm not exactly following your directions." I opened the laptop on my lap as if to show him what I had written and then closed it when I remembered that he was featured prominently in there. I looked at him and saw he was waiting for me to continue. I understood at that moment how Rosario might have confided in him. The guy was like a magnet for your deepest secrets. The rumor at school was that he had been a priest before leaving the church and becoming a teacher. Some said that he was excommunicated on account of the novel he wrote.

"What directions?"

"I know you told us that we should write in our journals knowing that no one would ever read what we write."

"Yes."

"But I'm writing my journal like a novel, hoping that it will be read by people, maybe even get published. If it's good enough." I thought I saw a tiny, tiny smile form across Mr. Cortazar's lips. I got the feeling he had heard those exact words from many kids before. There I was—just another wannabe writer.

"So, what do you put in your journal?"

"The things that I do. The stuff that happens to me. The

conversations I have with people. I write down dreams . . . sometimes."

"Mmm." Mr. Cortazar scratched his cheek, thinking. "Does that mean I have to watch what I say?"

"You can speak off the record." Sometimes I surprise myself with how quick and witty I am.

"Well, I suppose if you want to be a writer, a journal can be a training ground for writing a novel. But composing with an eye to be read may keep you from attaining one of the benefits of a journal—the self-knowledge it gives you."

"Self-knowledge?"

"We all have parts of us that we don't admit to anyone else. We don't even admit them to ourselves, usually. But if we are honest in our journals, those ugly parts will peep out and we can get to know them. That self-knowledge will make you a better person and a better writer. You will be able to give your characters the reality that only self-knowledge can give them. Can you do that with this novelistic journal you're writing?"

"Okay. I'll try. If I can ever find any ugly parts."

I got old man Cortazar to laugh. A first. Many have tried but few succeeded. "I'm sure you can come up with something," he said, composing himself. "Look. The practice of writing in a journal every day is just that: a practice. It's like a hundred free throws every day so that the foul shots can go in easily and effortlessly during the big game. The nice thing about practicing is that there's no pressure. You're just practicing. Don't turn the fun of practice into a pressure-packed game where everyone's watching and you want to shine."

I don't have time for no damn practice. My time may be running out. That's what I said to myself. To Mr. Cortazar I said: "What I'm doing seems to be working. Words are flowing."

"But are you being honest with yourself?" When he saw that I wasn't answering, he continued, "Well, I don't mean to put restrictions on what you're doing. Follow your inspiration wherever it takes you. It must be taking a lot of your time."

"A bit."

"Sometimes I see you nodding off in class. Do you work after school?"

"Before school. At the fish market."

Mr. Cortazar shook his head sadly. "There must be jobs out there with better hours."

Not many where I can make a couple of hundred a week selling weed, I thought. "I like it. I work with my friend Noah Santini. His father owns the store. Noah graduated from Stonebridge Charter a couple of years ago. I don't think he was in any of your classes. He was Rosario Zamora's boyfriend." I studied Mr. Cortazar's face to see his reaction to Rosario's name. He smiled to himself, the way one smiles when remembering something beautiful. "Rosario took your class," I said, probing further.

Mr. Cortazar inhaled deeply and then exhaled rapidly. "She did, she sure did." He took another deep breath. He was quiet for a long time. What he said next, he said to himself. I had the feeling he had forgotten I was there. "She was ambitious, like you."

"Ambitious?" It was a strange word to use, but it was also the perfect word to describe Rosario's dream to be a famous writer. She lived and breathed that dream since she read *A Separate Peace* in Mrs. Rivera's freshman English class. "Is that bad?"

Mr. Cortazar grimaced, as if the answer to that question was complicated. After a long pause, he said, "Writing is a lifelong project. As writers, we need to find a way to make writing part of our life and to keep doing it without the hope of a reward."

I know it was a mean thing to think, but I felt like saying, *Well, when it comes to your book, you certainly got your wish.* The joke around school was that Mr. Cortazar's novel had sold a hundred copies and Mr. Cortazar bought ninety-eight of them. Instead, I said, unable to hide the annoyance in my voice, "Rosario worked so hard to finish her book of short stories. Tons of times I'd see the light on in her apartment at four a.m. when I went to work at the fish market. I'd go in and find her at the kitchen table working on her book."

"Yes, I know she did." A change came over Mr. Cortazar's face. His eyes lost their focus and his head dropped as if defeated by the weight of memories. It was the mention of Rosario's short stories that took the living air out of him. I was sure of it. The old man felt something special for Rosario, I had no doubt. It was either guilt or love, I couldn't tell. I stared at him for a few seconds. I was about to ask him what he thought of Rosario's book when he snapped out of wherever he had gone and said, looking directly at me, "Tell me something. Why do you want to be a writer?"

I looked at him, surprised. I had never asked myself that question. "I want to be famous. Rich too. Money wouldn't hurt." Of all the possible answers, leave it to me say the first thing that came to my mouth.

Mr. Cortazar did not react to my answer. He said, "That may be why you want to publish a book. But why do you write? This journal that you're working on, why are you going beyond the requirements of the assignment?"

All I could think of was that that writing kept loneliness at a safe distance. I didn't say that. It sounded melodramatic even to my own ears. "I don't know," I finally said, "writing comes easy to me. I sit and the words come. I don't think about it that much." I felt like such an ignoramus just then. We spend hours in class looking at how people like Chekhov and George Saunders and other great writers carefully create their stories and there I was admitting to not thinking when I wrote. "Is that bad?" I asked guiltily.

"No," Mr. Cortazar said quickly. "It's not bad. It's very good. You're a natural. What that says to me is that you're writing your novel/journal as if it was a playful practice. Which is not to say that it is not a serious endeavor. That's good. Unusual. But at some point, the wind that's powering your sail will stop blowing, or maybe . . . you won't receive the recognition you hoped to receive . . ." Mr. Cortazar paused. I got the distinct impression he was thinking of Rosario. "Excuse me," he said, clearing his throat. "I lost my train of thought."

"If the wind that powers my sails stops blowing . . ."

"Yes," Mr. Cortazar said, smiling, "thank you. If the wind stops blowing, then you must row. If writing is your life, you'll keep at it. To be a writer, you'll need to find a way to make writing a practice, like the hundred free throws every day. That's why you do it. Writing will be a part of who you are, and you will write no matter what, easy or not easy, publishing or no publishing, acclaim or no acclaim." Mr. Cortazar looked away so that I would not see his eyes redden. He composed himself and said with his teacher's voice, "So, when do you hear from Sarah Lawrence?"

"Late March sometime."

"You sent in your financial aid application?"

"Yes. I forged my mother's signature. So it could be jail instead of college." Or it could be I'll be dead by this summer.

Mr. Cortazar didn't laugh. "You didn't tell your mother?"

"Nope."

"Why the secrecy?"

I shrugged. I didn't have an answer for his question. I probably could have dug up an answer if I tried, but I didn't want to talk about it. Going to college had been my dream since my sophomore year. But there and then, in front of Mr. Cortazar, the college dream lost all its juice.

Mr. Cortazar continued, "It's the perfect school if you want to learn how to write. I can make some calls."

"I don't know. College may not be in the cards for me."

"If it's because of money . . . there are scholarships."

I wanted to go back to talking about Rosario. What had

23

he read in Rosario's journal? Had he noticed anything wrong with her life, anything that the rest of us missed, that I missed? I was annoyed that Mr. Cortazar had deviated from Rosario to general platitudes about writing and then to the typical questions about college. "We'll see," I said.

After I left Mr. Cortazar, I went to the library, sat in front of one of the research terminals, and looked up Mr. Cortazar's book. The database showed that it had been checked out last May and never returned. I stood, walked up to the counter, and asked Mrs. Longoria if she had ever gone after the person who kept the book. She's a monster when it comes to retrieving overdue books. This time, she looked at me as if she were going to burst out crying. "I couldn't do that."

Not that I want to brag or anything, but I often get these hunches that turn out to be true. Like just then, I knew who had taken out Mr. Cortazar's book. "It was Rosario, wasn't it? She's the one who took out the book and never returned it."

Mrs. Longoria answered my question by turning around and hiding her face from me. I knew she was close to Rosario. Rosario had her own chair and table in the library, the same place where she ate lunch every day while reading a book. Mrs. Longoria grabbed a tissue, blew her nose loudly. She opened a drawer next to where she was sitting and took out a plastic container full of thick green liquid. That was the signal for me to disappear, but I stayed. I'm one of Mrs. Longoria's favorite students even if she doesn't know it—another one of those hunches that are true.

"What is it that you want? Ask it and be gone." Mrs. Longoria tried to sound angry but failed.

I hesitated, but only for the briefest of seconds. "So, have you read Mr. Cortazar's book?" I said to her.

"Yup," she said on the way back from the microwave in the office. She seemed surprised to see me standing in the same spot.

"What's it about? Mr. Cortazar's book."

Mrs. Longoria took a plastic spoon and a napkin with a flowery design on the edges out of a drawer. I smelled pea soup and bacon. My mouth watered. Mrs. Longoria spoke with the kind of tone you use when there is no other way of getting rid of someone. "I have the copy Tobias . . . Mr. Cortazar gave me. It's somewhere. Or ask Mr. Cortazar for a copy. I'm sure he's got a few lying around."

"Come on, give me the elevator version and I'm out of here."

Mrs. Longoria stood and disappeared into her office. A few minutes later, she came back with a paperback that looked as if it had never been opened. "Go read the book," Mrs.

Longoria said, sitting down again. "Now let me eat my lunch in peace. Scoot. Go. Bye. Adios."

The title of Mr. Cortazar's book was *The Tiger's Path*. It had a sleek-looking tiger, red eyes shining, coming out of a tunnel. The book had been printed in 1995. I did the math in my head. Assuming Mr. Cortazar was sixty or so, the book was published when he was in his thirties.

"Okay, okay." I walked to the desk where I had been sitting and dropped the book in my backpack. On my way out, I stopped in front of Mrs. Longoria and waited for her to finish chewing. "I need to ask you a serious question." I knew it was impossible for her not to respond to a serious question by a student. It was just impossible. So, I blurted out what I should have asked Mr. Cortazar but didn't have the courage to. "Did you notice anything different . . . about Rosario . . . when she checked the book out? Or before that?"

Mrs. Longoria pushed her bowl away. There was still soup in there, but I had a feeling she would not be able to continue eating. She took out a blue tissue from a box and blew her nose. When she was finally able to lift her eyes and look at me, she said, "No, I didn't notice anything, not really. She was quieter than usual, I guess. She sat at her usual table with her laptop open, looking out the window. I thought she was just bored of school like every senior I know. Whatever was going on in her head had either not started or was contained. Sealed up. I remember making a joke about how she would be one of three humans who had read Tobias's book, and she didn't hear me or even respond to me. She was someplace else. Do you know what happened to Rosario? I sure don't." I started to answer but she cut me off. "Not that it matters anymore. What's done is done."

But it does matter. Yes, it does.

Thursday, February 2

During school days, my hours at the fish market are from four a.m. to six a.m. When school is out, I go full tilt from two a.m. to seven a.m. What I do there is lug, lug, lug. I lug ice from the ice machine to the stalls. I lug boxes of fish from trucks and into trucks, sometimes with a fork-lift and sometimes with an "ass-lift," as Sal calls it. Salvatore Santini and his son Noah are the owners of Santini and Son Fish Wholesaler, an enterprise first established by Sal's great-grandfather back when the Fulton Fish Market was still in lower Manhattan.

To get to the market by four, I need to get out the door of our apartment by three thirty. I walk down Edgewater Road still half asleep in the hope that some trucker going down to the market will see me trudging in the cold and give me a ride. At two a.m. there's never a problem getting a ride, but by four a.m. most of the truck traffic is going in the opposite direction. This morning the snow was flying sideways off the Bronx River and tiny icicles were forming on my eyelashes. I was pushing against a gust of wind, trying to remember what Rosario said in my dream, when I heard the life-saving roar of Noah's 1969 GTO.

"Damn, it's cold," I said, rubbing my hands and looking to see how I could crank up the heat.

"All this time working with dead fish and you still not used to cold," Noah said. He was smoking a cigarette and had the driver's window rolled halfway down. He put the gearshift into first and the car rumbled slowly forward.

"Where we going? I asked, when Noah made a U-turn.

"Sal closed early. I'm taking you home."

"That's a first."

"It's gonna blizzard all day. Restaurants are canceling orders."

A woman protecting herself from the wind inside a door-way shouted something. Noah stopped the car and motioned for me to roll down my window. "Need a ride?" Noah asked the woman.

The woman had on tight black leather pants and a fake-fur jacket. She made her way to my window and leaned her head all the way in. Her shoulder-length blonde hair was wet and raggedy. "Would you give me a ride to the subway? I'll pay you like an Uber."

"Get in," Noah said.

She opened the passenger door and I moved forward so she could climb into the back seat, but she sat next to me. "Scoot over, babe, unless you want me to sit on your lap." Her voice sounded young. Our legs were touching when I finally made it to the middle. Noah rolled up his window and then opened it a crack again.

"You working tonight?" Noah asked.

"No, I'm out here for the view." I turned to look at her. She was rubbing her left arm and shivering. She was twentysomething, I guessed.

"My buddy here's a virgin. Maybe you can cut him a deal?" Noah said, elbowing me and laughing.

When I turned in her direction, my eyes met hers. She had the palest blue eyes I had ever seen. She looked deeply into me and I had a strange feeling of something once beautiful but quickly fading.

"What you think?" Noah asked.

"Cut it out, man," I said, irritated. I could tell the woman was not in a joking mood.

"No. I'm not messing with him." The way she said it, it made me feel the opposite of rejected, as if I would awaken feelings in her she didn't want awakened. That's the interpretation I chose to give to her words, but who knows? I grabbed my backpack from under my feet and took out one of the baggies of weed cigarettes I sold at the fish market. I knew I would have to make up the twenty dollars to the X-Tecas somehow, but I didn't care. It seemed like the right thing to do at that moment.

"Here," I said. "For you."

"What? Wow, thank you!" She took out a tiny purple purse from a pocket in her fur coat and started to open it. "Let me pay you for this and for the ride."

"The ride's on us," Noah said.

"And the weed's on me," I said.

"Well, what do ya know? Just when you think is all bleak." Noah pulled up next to the entrance to the subway. She opened the door to get out and then she closed it and extended her hand to me. "I'm Mimi," she said.

I shook her hand. "Nico."

"I seen you walking to the market some nights," she said, letting go of my hand. "Stop by and say hi sometime."

"What about me?" Noah shouted.

"You? I don't do drunks," Mimi said, laughing and pointing with her chin at the bottle of vodka next to him. She shut the door and rushed down into the subway entrance.

Noah looked in the mirror and then made a screeching U-turn. I breathed in the smell of burning rubber. "You got yourself a girlfriend," Noah joked.

"How old you think she is?"

"It's hard to tell with heroin addicts. Every year you use adds ten to how you look. She's around twenty-five, I'd say."

"How you know she's a heroin addict?"

"The way she rubbed her arms. And, think about it, why would anyone as smart as her be out on a night like this?"

"How you know she's smart?"

"She didn't want to mess with you." Noah held off laughing until he couldn't.

"Funny. You're a regular stand-up comic." I thought for a few moments and then said: "Why would a smart person try heroin?"

Noah slowed down and looked at me. He knew I was

thinking of Rosario. He took out a cigarette, turned onto Spofford Avenue, found a space where the streetlight was broken, and stopped the car. He reached next to him and grabbed the bottle of vodka. It was the expensive Russian kind, which Noah claimed was better for your liver.

Noah reached over and took out two paper cups from the glove compartment. He poured a finger's worth of vodka into my glass and about three fingers into his. Then he fiddled with the station until he found a classic rock station. He took a long drag from his cigarette and blew the smoke out his half-open window. "Sal's worried about me. The drinking." He raised his paper cup. "And he's afraid I'm going to leave him for a better job. He'd like to retire someday and leave the business to me, but he's worried the job may be too tough. Hell, he's afraid to lose you too. Where's he gonna find another fool that gets up at three a.m. for eleven bucks an hour? That's why he tolerates your little side gig there." Noah glanced down at my backpack.

"He knows?"

"He's no dummy."

"It's a helluva job," I said. "The hours, the bags of ice, the lifting, the stinking fish staring at you like you're responsible for their demise."

Noah laughed, then said, "The only way to work that job is if you have someone waiting for you in the morning when you get home."

"Yeah."

We were quiet, listening to Freddie Mercury sing "Bohemian Rhapsody," when Noah said, "That song kills me." He exhaled. "To answer your question about why a smart person would try heroin. I thought about it. What I tell myself is she tried it and figured she could control it. For a while maybe she was in control. Just enjoying the high. Then it went sideways."

"Yeah? You think so?" There was hope in my voice. I too wanted to believe that Rosario's death was a horrible mistake.

"What I tell myself is she didn't know how much or where. None of that."

"You didn't notice . . ."

"Nothing. The breakdown was after me. Listen, last time she and me were together . . . was that Saturday, day of her graduation. She seemed out of it . . . but . . . there's no way she was using then."

"Then she broke up with you a few days after. Why?" Maybe it was the dream I had that was giving me strength to finally ask.

Noah drank whatever vodka was in his paper cup. "Around a month before, must have been early May, she started pulling away. She didn't wanna do anything, go out to dinner, nothin'. Didn't want me to come over. Said she wanted to work on her book. By the time she told me she wanted break up, it . . . I already knew I lost her. What I figure is, I was lucky to be with her for a year. She was out of my league . . . as they say."

I looked at Noah with a glint of admiration. You'd never know it by looking at him, but underneath his rough exterior there was something tender and gentle and fragile. I'm sure those were the qualities that attracted Rosario to him even if I never believed he could be Rosario's soul mate. "Was there someone else, you think?" I wished I didn't sound as guilty as I did.

Noah glared at me momentarily. Then he said, "Alma told me you were asking about Rosario and Mr. Cortazar. Rosario used to talk about his class all the time. She told me once it was her most favorite class out of the whole four years." Noah took a deep breath and closed his eyes as if to remember better. After a long while he said, "Mr. Cortazar was helping her with the book of stories. He was probably in love with her. Like you." Noah gave me one of his scary, piercing looks. I'm pretty sure he could hear my heart thump against my chest. I was an open window and Noah could see all of me. I made a gesture with my eyes and hands as if to say "Busted!" Then he laughed. Relieved, I laughed as well. He unscrewed the top of the vodka bottle and poured himself another three fingers. He didn't even offer to pour any into my cup. I hadn't drunk any of my vodka. Noah never gave me more than was needed to warm up. He put the bottle by his side and said, a serious tone to his voice, "She was used to people crushing on her. Cortazar never stepped over any line, far as I know."

"And Rosario? How did she feel about him?"

Noah gave me one of his *why are you asking dumb questions* looks. Nevertheless, he chose to answer. "He took her writing seriously, man. You're a writer, you know how that makes you feel." There was long pause, then, "He was the last person she talked to. She called him from that motel in Queens."

"What? I didn't know that. Does Alma know this?"

"She's the one who told me." Noah gulped the rest of his vodka, threw the cup out the window, rolled the window back up. He turned the car's lights on and placed his hand on the stick shift. "Let's go home. I'm beat."

"Bro, wait, what? You gotta fill me in here."

Noah gripped the black steering wheel with both hands.

Without looking at me, he said, "Alma checked Rosario's phone, a few days after . . . and there was a twenty-minute call to Mr. Cortazar."

"Did Alma . . ."

"Yeah, she did. Alma asked Mr. Cortazar."

"And?"

"It was about her book of short stories. She was calling him for updates."

"Okay, and?"

"Cortazar told Rosario he hadn't heard back from the place they sent the story."

"It took twenty minute to tell her? No way!" I was angry just then. I was angry at Alma, at Noah, at Mr. Cortazar, even at Rosario. I felt like I had been left out of something important. Noah put the car in first and drove into the empty street. He drove in silence. When he parked in front of my apartment building, he said, "What you so pissed about?"

"I can't believe you guys didn't tell me anything."

"Look, it was Alma's information to share and she shared it with me. If you weren't so blind to how she feels about you maybe she would trust you too."

I grabbed the sides of my head. I couldn't believe what I had just heard. "She is going out with Ruben, the second-in-command for the X-Tecas. She *chose* to be with him. What does that tell you about her feelings for me?"

"Yeah, well, she's only going out with him cause you're blind."

"I'm not!"

"Blind as a mogul."

"A mogul?"

"One of them animals that can't see. They look like possums but without the long tail and they're brown."

"Mole?" I tried not to laugh, but it wasn't possible. We both laughed one of those tears-coming-out-of-your-eyes-and-nose kind of laughs. When we stopped, I felt a heavy, wet kind of sadness. It was true. One of those truths that gnawed at me for a long time. I had hurt Alma. Somewhere along the line she had offered me more than friendship and I had rejected her offer.

"What should I do?" I asked Noah.

"Do you like her . . . like that?"

"Not like that. I mean, I can see that she's attractive, but she's a friend . . . like you."

"Uh . . . I ain't *that* kind of friend . . ."

"Oh, hell. What does it matter? It's not something I need

to figure out before this summer." I grabbed my backpack and opened the door.

"What's happening this summer?"

"A dream is coming true," I said enigmatically. "Later."

When I looked back, Noah was crouching and had his palms stretched like he was still waiting for an explanation.

Friday, February 3

I woke up to a strange sound in the living room. Julia was asleep on the sofa, a gurgling noise coming out of her throat. She had turned on the television and then fallen asleep. It was almost nine. Later than Julia ever slept. I placed a cushion under her head and turned off the TV. I walked across the hall to Alma's apartment and paused when I remembered what Noah had said to me: *If you weren't so blind to how she feels about you maybe she would trust you too.* Then Alma opened the door. "What are you doing standing there?"

"How you know I was here?"

"I could hear you breathing all the way inside."

And there she was in front of me. The right girl, according

to Noah and to Julia and to Rosario. But for some strange reason, not according to my heart. Alma was beautiful. I could see how she could take someone's breath away and maybe someday I would understand why I wasn't one of the breathless ones.

"Stop it!" Alma said as I followed her in.

"Stop what?" I entered and immediately searched the living room and kitchen to see if Ruben was there.

"Whatever you were thinking just then. It wasn't nice." Alma headed to the kitchen. I noticed she was wearing those extremely tight jeans of hers. "And stop staring at my butt! What's the matter with you today?"

"Nothing," I said, embarrassed. I walked over and peered into the pot that Alma was stirring. Sopa de fideos con carne. The smell made my mouth water.

"Sit down and I'll give you a bowl. It's almost done."

"You make it?" I sat down and tore off a piece from a baguette on the table.

"Mami. I'm just reheating."

"You walking to school or is Ruben picking you up?"

"Neither. Staying home with Pepito. He's got an ear infection. Another one." Alma filled two bowls with the noodles and meat, took out two spoons, and sat down next to me.

She tore off a piece of bread and started eating. "So? What's bugging you this time?" I got up, opened the refrigerator, and took out the bottle of hot sauce. Alma watched me shake the bottle five times over my bowl. "Mexicans," she said.

"Man, your mom can cook." I slurped a spoonful of fideos. Alma was grabbing a piece of meat from her bowl and sticking it inside her bread. I did the same.

When she finished chewing, she said, "You gonna be late."

"Independent Research, first period," I said with my mouth full. When I finished chewing, I said casual-like: "Noah told me something kinda disturbing yesterday."

"Uh-oh. Here it comes."

"What?"

"I knew something was bugging you. You're weirder than usual today."

I shut my eyes and took a deep breath. "How come you never told me about Rosario's call to Mr. Cortazar. The last one she made?"

Alma kept on eating as if I wasn't there. Finally, she pushed her plate away and said, looking straight at me, "One, because you would jump to all kinds of wrong conclusions. And two, because . . . you already have too much Rosario on your mind."

"What does that mean?" I asked, indignant.

"Let's drop it, okay? Why is all this talk about Rosario coming up now?"

Could I tell Alma about my dream and the part Rosario played in it without getting her even more angry at me?

"Tell me," Alma insisted.

"I had a dream," I gushed. "It was a complicated dream. So damn real. Rosario was in it." I waited nervously for Alma's reaction.

Alma sighed. I took that as permission to forge ahead.

"It was the night after we had that conversation about Rosario and Mr. Cortazar. You know, the journal thing." Alma wrinkled her nose—her way of letting me know she remembered. "I was in a coffin in Mr. Ortiz's funeral parlor. Rosario was there. She said something to me. But when I woke up, I couldn't remember."

A flicker of anger crossed Alma's face. "She came all the way back to earth to tell you exactly what?"

"Come on, don't be like that. The whole thing felt like some kind of message. The dream has me rattled. My head's full of questions."

"Like?"

"Why did she spiral out of control like that? What caused her to self-destruct? What happened to her?"

"And you think she's asking you to find out?" It had been a very long time since I'd seen Alma so angry. I waited until she unlocked her eyes from mine and looked away.

It had not occurred to me until that moment that Rosario was asking something of me in that dream—was she asking something that somehow would make a difference in my life? What did Rosario lose that I had to keep? I looked up and saw Alma waiting for a response. "Could be," I said.

Alma ran a hand through her brown hair. "I don't want to return to those days. Rosario broke. People break. She broke from the inside, not from something outside. Maybe some from the outside."

"Don't we see cracks before people break? It wasn't like Rosario to give up on life."

"And you know this because, of course, you knew her better than anyone!"

I wanted to say that, in a way, yes, maybe I did know Rosario better than anyone. Instead, I asked, "Don't you think it's important to know the truth?"

"Why is it so important now?"

"I told you . . . that dream . . ."

"Why that dream now? Rosario's been dead for almost six months. How she died wasn't eating at you back then."

44

Is there a timing for dreams? Do they come out like plants when the soil is just right and they can get properly noticed? I was surprised, shocked even, when I heard that Rosario had been found dead from an apparent overdose of heroin. But Alma was right, the *why* did not eat at me then the way it did now. "Maybe it hurt too much, back then, to ask why" is what I managed to say.

"I don't want to go back to that hurt," Alma said firmly. "And you shouldn't either. There were cracks in Rosario's life that you don't know. Mental traumas she hid. She wasn't happy with all this." Alma extended her arms and I understood that "this" meant their apartment in Hunts Point and beyond. "Let her be, okay?"

"Okay," I said. She was asking me not to cause her any more pain. I understood. I stood and went over to her. I bent down and kissed her on top of her head. "I'm sorry," I said.

I didn't need to say all that I was sorry about. Alma knew.

Saturday, February 4

I'm thinking that it was around this time last year when Rosario started to unravel. Now I'm looking for clues that it was happening. How did I miss the cracks in Rosario's life that Alma says were there?

I remember one afternoon watching Pepito while Alma went to the store. Pepito was asleep in the living room and when I picked up a magazine from the coffee table, a brochure for Sarah Lawrence College fell on the floor. I knew it belonged to Rosario so I walked to her room, glad for the excuse to talk to her. She was at her desk typing. I handed it to her. She glanced at it, took it from me without a word, and went back to typing.

"Did you apply?" I asked Rosario.

Rosario looked around as if to make sure no one else was in the room. "Nope." She closed her laptop so I couldn't see what she was writing. "What are you doing here, Nicolás? Where's Alma? Scoot. I'm busy."

I ignored both her words and the flicking motion of her fingers. "Why? Why not college?"

Just then Mrs. Zamora shouted from her room. "Rosario, those dishes ain't gonna get done by themselves! I don't wanna come home to a dirty kitchen!"

"Why not college? That's why." Rosario pointed with her thumb in the direction of where the shouting had come. Then, lowering her voice: "Can you believe she's going on a date? Not Pepito's father, someone else."

"It's not fair. You're too smart not to go to college." I sat down on the edge of a pink easy chair next to her desk, poking at her aggravation, hoping she'd keep talking to me. It worked. Rosario got her legs out from under the desk, pushed her chair back, and faced me.

"My dear mother. Three kids by three different fathers. Not one of them ever paid child support. Each father worse than the last."

"Pepito's father seemed all right."

47

"He was *not!*" They were only three words, but they were spoken with an intensity that scared me.

"Hey," I said after a long silence, "your mother can be a character in one of your stories."

"She's probably a character in all my stories in one form or another."

"I mean, you gotta admit, your mother *is* a character. She's got looks. Like her daughter."

Rosario looked at me in a way that let me know she knew what I was up to. "Like her daughters," Rosario corrected me. "Alma is the true beauty in this family, Nicolás. Get it through your head."

"So," I said, quickly, changing the subject, "if not college, then what?"

"Writing, writing, writing. I'm almost ready to send out my book of short stories. Next, an agent. A publishing contract. Then I'm out of Hunts Point. In Manhattan if the advance is big enough. Otherwise, someplace nice. But out of here. The next book—a novel—will be big. I have an outline." She stopped. I saw her lip quiver. When she spoke again, she wasn't speaking to me anymore. "That's the way it will happen. I'm not spending the rest of my life working at Lushy Foods." She made her voice sound like a male TV announcer:

"'Our specialty, all natural, grass-fed, and non-GMO protein products. We specialize in good-quality offal.'"

"Rosario, I ain't foolin'!" Mrs. Zamora shouted.

She looked at me as if I were the one yelling at her. "No college for me, Nicolás. It's Lushy Foods selling offal for a few months and then I'm going to do something extraordinary with my life. I'll be somebody." She stood. "Someday soon. Right now, the dirty dishes!"

Was your anger a sign that you would eventually give up on life, Rosario? Help me understand the path you took. Because if anger at the dirty dishes in your life was a step on the road to self-destruction, what hope is there for the rest of us?

Sunday, February 5

The dirty dishes in our life? Here's one of mine: Javier. Julia asked me to go out and look for him. It was eleven p.m. and he wasn't home. I went over to Hunts Point playground. Primo and three other X-Tecas were leaning against the handball court. They were smoking weed and passing around a bottle of cheap wine. All four of them had on these identical gray hoodies that were not nearly thick enough to keep them warm.

Primo stood slowly and walked toward me. He had an almost unnoticeable limp that made him seem as if he had all the time in the world. "What's up?" he asked, as if I were an old friend.

"Looking for Javier."

"He's probably at the house playing video games." Primo turned to one of the other X-Tecas. "Call Javier and tell him to go home."

"Thanks," I said. By *house* I knew Primo was referring to the X-Tecas headquarters on Gilbert Place. I thought for a moment of walking away, but Primo had a presence that was hard to walk away from. It wasn't menacing or anything. It was more like something in you wanted to please him. I knew that Javier was closer to Primo than to any other human being. I walked up to Primo and said, mustering courage, "Javier, he's just a kid. He should be home. With us. My mother and me. She worries." I tried not to sound either afraid or threatening. With the X-Tecas, it was all about speaking with a combination of courage and respect—a difficult art I'm not sure I had fully mastered.

Primo grinned almost as if he were feeling sorry for my naivete. Primo was one of those well-built, chiseled-face guys who seemed out of place as an ex-convict or the leader of a gang. "Come on," he said politely, pointing to a bench a few feet from the handball court. "Let's talk." Primo wore these ankle-high boots with a steel plate on the right foot to make up for the fact that one leg was shorter than the other. He invited me to sit down on the bench. He sat next to me and offered me a cigarette.

"No, thanks." I was nervous and suspicious of his unexpected courtesy. All my encounters with Primo before had never lasted more than five minutes. Five minutes that felt like an hour. I tried to stay calm. Primo had the confidence of a man who had survived ten years of prison life. He was also smart, which only made him more dangerous in my eyes.

"Listen, Nico. I don't know what kind of deal you made with Ruben, but I'm the only one who makes deals for us. Do you understand?"

I thought I heard a threat in the way he asked if I understood. I nodded. He continued.

"I have an idea. You work at the fish market. You know the delivery guys that distribute fish to the restaurants and bars all over the city, Manhattan, Brooklyn, Queens. Find us . . . three, let's start with three. Three drivers who can take our merchandise and sell it wherever they're located. You do that and I'm thinking you'll be clearing five, ten thousand a month. Couldn't you use the money?"

Could I use the money? I could give the money to Julia and

go to college guilt-free. Or maybe getting involved with the X-Tecas was how my funeral dream would come true. "What about Javier?" I asked. But Primo could see I was already hooked by his proposal.

Primo made a face as if to say, *There's nothing to be done about Javier.* "No way I can keep him away from us, the kid wants to be blood. If it's not us, it'll be some other. But I'll take care of him. I'll make sure he stays out of juvie."

"I'll think about it," I said. I tried to stand but Primo held my arm.

"Sit down, sit down. Listen, listen to me. This merchandise that I want you to transport is coke and maybe some molly. Party stuff, that's all. Stuff the drivers can unload easy in their fancy bars and restaurants. No big deal. Cops aren't even busting people for that anymore. You already in with us selling weed, so we can say you got one foot in the game, right?"

I didn't answer. I kept my eyes on the steel plate in his right boot. Primo had turned his disability into a weapon. There was a part of me that wanted to say yes right there and then. Javier was a lost cause, why not admit it? And Primo was right, I was already ankle deep in the drug business. "Only coke and ecstasy?" I asked.

"Yeah, man. La pura verdad." Here Primo made a cross with his thumb and index finger and kissed it.

"I'll look into it. I may know some drivers." I said, standing up.

He stood as well. "Cool, man, cool. Someone like you could be a real help to us."

"Someone like me."

"You're not like those guys." He pointed at the X-Tecas by the handball courts. "You're smart. You got it together. You going places. We need vatos like you. Give us a good face. Not to be in our clica. Like independent contractors, know what I'm sayin?"

There was something in Primo's tone that made me feel special. Like he really knew me and would take care of me. Dealing drugs for the X-Tecas. I could see a shine to it. Being successful at it in a way that those "other guys" could never be.

Primo put his arm around my shoulder. "Find us some drivers. After you make your connections and make enough money, you can stop. You can stop anytime and go on with your life. I know you got plans. Think about my proposition, Nicolás. Let me know soon."

His use of my name shook me. Only one person ever called

me by my full name: Rosario. The mention of my full name on the lips of Primo made me realize I was the person I wanted Rosario to see and love and not the person Primo saw. I took a few steps back and said, "No, thanks."

Then I turned around and walked away.

Monday, February 6

I was in front of my locker, trying to open a combination lock that never opens on the first try, when someone tapped me on the shoulder. I turned around and saw Ruth Silvester. She was wearing black pants and a black turtleneck sweater. When I noticed she had the same pearl earrings as in my dream, I jumped back, terrified, which caused Ruth to jump back as well.

"I'm so sorry, I didn't mean to startle you," she stammered.

"No, no. It's okay. I was daydreaming. You surprised me."

In all the analysis of the dream that I had done since the night it occurred, I had never questioned Ruth's presence at my funeral. Ruth was a senior like me. She and I had shared several classes through the years, and she wanted to be a writer too, but she wasn't someone I would expect to show up at my funeral. Ruth, by the way, fit all the stereotypes of a genius: extremely shy, afraid to look you in the eyes, hardly ever spoke, and when she did it was as if she fully expected you to laugh at her. Algebra, one of the classes we shared our first year of high school was like child's play to her. Lots of times I saw her finish a test twenty minutes ahead of everyone else and just sit there quietly until the bell rang. I was under the impression that she was on her way to discover the cure for cancer. But when Mr. Cortazar went around on the first day of class asking us why we wanted to take a creative writing course, Ruth astounded us all by saying she was working on a fantasy novel. The one thing about Ruth: It was impossible to envy her or resent her brilliance. She was so beyond the orbit of everyone at Stonebridge Charter that envying her would be like getting angry at Shakespeare for writing *Hamlet* before you could come up with it. She was also the reason why the Stonebridge Charter Math Club was first place in the city.

Ruth clutched her laptop to her chest. "I have a question to ask you."

"Sure, sure. Hold on." I tried the combination one more

time and this time the door to my locker opened. I noticed that Ruth had taken a step back. She was looking at the floor sadly, just like in my dream. I grabbed my green army-surplus coat and my backpack and then turned to face Ruth. Her short red hair was parted on one side and I could see a blue vein pulsing in her temple.

She took a deep breath and said with pretend confidence: "The taco truck is out front today. Would you like a taco?"

"A taco?" I started to walk in the direction of the exit.

Ruth hesitated and then kept up with me. "Yes. I need a favor. Something to do with writing."

We stepped outside and raised our hands to shield our eyes from the sun. It seemed months since I'd last felt the sun. The light was good but it was still cold. I zipped up my coat and Ruth put on the fluffy red parka she was carrying in her arms.

"Hey," I said, "want to have a cup of coffee or tea at Cholo's? I'm not much of a taco guy, even though I'm half Mexican."

"Yes, that would be better."

We went down the stairs. Out in the street I saw Alma get into Ruben's black SUV.

"Are you any good at interpreting dreams?" I couldn't believe I actually asked her that.

Ruth seemed startled by my question. "I know that in a dream, nothing is as it seems. Everything is a symbol."

"This dream I had was so real. It felt . . . it feels like it was telling me something."

"Like Joseph."

"Who?"

"Joseph in the Bible. He interprets Pharaoh's dream to mean there will be seven years of famine."

"And does the famine come? I'm not much of a Bible reader."

Ruth gave me a small grin of understanding before answering. "No. They store grain and prevent famine, thanks to Joseph's dream. They change the outcome."

I thought, *If Rosario is beckoning, I don't want to change the outcome.*

"Are you okay?"

Ruth's voice brought me back to the present. It occurred to me that even though this was the longest conversation I'd ever had with Ruth, I felt totally comfortable talking to her and telling her about my dream. It was almost as if the fact that she had shown up in my dream made her an emotional accomplice of sorts. I then proceeded to tell Ruth Silvester my dream with every single detail I could remember. The only thing I left out was her presence. I thought that would be too scary for her. By the time I finished we were at the entrance to Cholo's. As usual, the place was full of boisterous grade school kids from the public school next door. Ruth had jasmine tea and I had a triple espresso. The sudden warmth of the coffee shop turned Ruth's ears and nose bright red. All the tables were occupied, but there was a bench by the front window. We moved the magazines and sat there. Ruth was deep in thought. She had listened to my dream with a serious kind of attention and I was sure she was now thinking about it.

"I had Rosario in my trigonometry class," Ruth said, remembering. "She was the only junior in the class. The rest of us were sophomores."

I felt a warmth in my heart at Ruth's mention of Rosario. "I told her not to take that class. She wanted to be a writer. What was she doing taking trigonometry? And then she takes calculus her senior year! And she did well in them! I scraped by algebra with a C-minus."

Ruth chuckled. Then, raising her voice slightly so I could hear her: "You must be close to her if she appears in your dreams."

I looked at her, wondering why she used the present tense. "She died last year. A month after graduation."

Ruth nodded. "But you're still close to her."

I looked at Ruth the way you look at someone who finally understands what you feel. I waited for the wave of sadness to pass and then I asked, "You know . . . about how she died?"

"Yes," she said softly. Then she added, "I believe dreams speak to us if we listen. There's a meaning you must discover . . . for the image of your death . . . and for why Rosario came to you . . ."

The way Ruth said this, I suddenly understood why she was in my dream. She and I were going to be friends. "Yes, yes. That's what I think too. I feel it more than anything. Thank you for listening and . . . taking me seriously. I'm sorry for dumping on you like this. But you had a question for me."

"Oh, I'm not sure this . . ."

"Yes, it is. It's the right time. It was a big help to tell you my dream and all. So now ask your question."

"Well . . . there's this book I've been working on. It's big. It's a fantasy and it's four hundred pages. I was going to ask you if you'd be interested in it."

"You're done already? Yeah, you said you were working on

it in class. But, wow, you finished! Yes, the answer is yes. I'm happy to read your novel. Send it to me."

"Are you sure? You have so much on your mind right now."

"Yes, I'm sure. I'm not all that much into fantasy—but it'll be fun."

"It's not very original. You'll see that I borrow most of it from Tolkien and other fantasy writers. I just wanted a format that would help me practice writing. Are you working on something? You're the only other person in our class who wants to be a writer."

"Me? No. Just the journal that Mr. Cortazar assigned to us. It's kind of novelesque. A journal on steroids. How exciting can that be?" I laughed; Ruth didn't. She seemed more interested in how I said things than in what I was saying. I continued. "I feel this urgency about it. After that dream especially. Like it's more important than ever that I finish before . . ."

I expected Ruth to say that the meaning of my dream was not literal, that it was not a prediction of my death this summer, but she didn't, and I was grateful for that. I saw her struggling, deciding whether to say out loud what she was thinking. Finally, she said, trying to keep her eyes on mine, her face turning bright red as she spoke: "Your wish to write is a gift. You need to honor it."

I tried to think of something funny to say, something that would lessen Ruth's obvious embarrassment, but for the first time in a very long time, I had no words, funny or otherwise. I remembered Rosario saying something similar about her wish to be a writer—it was a gift that was also a terrible burden to her.

Sometimes it happens that you accidentally enter a closeness with someone, a closeness that neither one expected. I think that's what happened with Ruth and me right then. I stepped out of that moment and said, "What are you doing next year?" Rumor around school was that she had gotten invitations to apply for early admission to Princeton, Yale, and Harvard.

Ruth turned her mug slightly so that the handle faced her. I glimpsed pain in her eyes. The noise from the kids got even louder so I stood and motioned that we should go outside.

When we walked out of Cholo's it started to snow. Ruth and I walked to the corner in silence and then she said she had to go left.

She hesitated and then said, "To answer your question, I'm not sure what I will do next year. My parents would like me to go to medical school. My father is a physician, and my mother is a nurse. They run the urgent care on Southern Boulevard. I got into some schools with good premed programs. But I also applied early action to Sarah Lawrence College, and I found out at the end of December that I was accepted."

"You did? Wow! Congratulations. Mr. Cortazar made me fill out an application for Sarah Lawrence as well."

"You should be hearing from them soon."

"I don't know. I'm not sure it's possible."

"Because of your dream?"

"And my situation at home." *My dirty dishes*, I said to myself.

"I need to decide soon. Your opinion of my novel will help me."

"Oof. Wow. My opinion. Geez. I'm not sure I'm a good judge of . . ."

"All you need to do is be honest with me. Please!"

Part of me felt like I was being unfairly pressed for honesty on all sides. There was Mr. Cortazar's push for honesty in writing and now here was Ruth demanding it from me and basing so much on me providing it. "Okay," I said tentatively, "I can be honest." *But if the novel stinks, I'll lie a little.*

The sunshine I'd felt earlier was covered by a dark cloud and wind was blowing snow into Ruth's face. Her nose began to run and she wiped it with the sleeve of her jacket. "Oh, when you get it, you'll see the name Briel Alexander on the cover. It's me. I decided to use a pseudonym."

"Why?" I asked. "Aren't you proud of your novel?"

"It's not that. Knowing I would use a pseudonym helped me, as I was writing, to concentrate on the work, to make sure it was about the story itself and the characters and not about me, worrying about or wishing what others might think of me. Does that make sense?"

"Like Mr. Cortazar says we should write our journal—not expecting anyone to read it."

"Yeah," she said. "Like that. Thanks again, Nico."

I watched her walk down the side street and for a few moments I was filled with a warm, grateful feeling. I tried to remember where I had recently felt that, and it came to me that it was like Rosario's presence in my dream.

Tuesday, February 7

Julia pulled down her brown wool hat so that it covered her ears and sped up a little. She coughed a few times and then said, "We're gonna be late again."

We were on our way to see Mr. Mallard, the principal of Javier's school. "Let me get us a car," I suggested.

"It's only ten blocks. We don't have money for cars."

Money and the lack of it was constantly on Julia's mind. Javier's father had not sent a single child support payment for the past four years. Getting Fernando Rojas to pay up was always a huge bureaucratic, legal, and emotional battle that Julia had to go through every few months. It took a lot out of her to visit social services agencies, hire cheap lawyers, and confront Fernando, who was not an easy person to confront. I think one of the reasons Julia started going out with Harrison was because he was a paralegal in a small law firm in Pelham. Unfortunately, Harrison turned out to be a real estate paralegal and an opioid addict. But he was kind to Julia, and he brought a big bag of groceries whenever he came to the house.

This was the third time this year that Julia had been summoned to meet with Mr. Mallard about problems with Javier. It was always an unpleasant experience for everyone and the fact that we got there at five minutes before five, when everyone was on their way out, only made things worse. Julia was out of breath and coughing and Mr. Mallard sat behind his desk, looking at his watch, waiting for her to stop. The son of a bitch couldn't even offer her a glass of water from the cooler outside his office. I got up and got her some in one of those cone paper cups. When she finished drinking the water, I crumpled the cup and stuck it in my pocket. What I wanted to do was toss it in the guy's impatient face.

"I'm sorry we're late," Julia said. Then, looking at me, "We shoulda taken a car."

"I'll get straight to the point, Mrs. Rojas." Mr. Mallard leaned forward and tapped his desk with his finger.

"Lozano. My last name is Lozano."

Mr. Mallard opened a brown file and read. "Javier Rojas is your son, correct?"

This was the third time that we had gone through the same rigamarole with the last names. Julia Lozano, mother of Nico Kardos and Javier Rojas, how hard can that be? Julia continued, explaining, "I was never married to Fernando . . . Javier's father, but Fernando wanted Javier to have his last name."

Mr. Mallard shook his head in a sanctimonious-judgment way. I was ready to tell the bastard where to get off when Julia elbowed me. "It's all right," she whispered. "It can be confusing."

"What is not confusing is that Javier broke another student's nose. Honestly, Mrs. Rojas, we're at our wit's end with your son. The parents of the student with the broken nose are threatening to press charges. If that happens, Javier may end up in a juvenile detention facility."

"Who started it?" I asked.

"It doesn't matter who started it. We have zero tolerance for violence in the school." The man practically had steam coming out of his ears.

Julia elbowed me again, but I ignored her. "It does too matter. Javier could have been defending himself. What were the circumstances? Was it a fight? Did Javier just walk up to the kid and punch him in the nose? These details matter."

"My son is . . ." Julia started to speak, but Mr. Mallard interrupted. He looked like he wanted to jump over the desk and grab me by the throat.

"Those kinds of details do not matter when it's your brother's third act of violence this year!" He shifted his angry eyes from me to Julia and said, raising his voice, "Your son is emotionally disturbed."

Mr. Mallard's office was surrounded on three sides by glass and the two women who worked outside were peering in, concerned looks on their faces.

Julia waited for Mr. Mallard to calm down. She spoke in a hoarse whisper, trying not to cough. "If Javier is sent to jail, he will come out worse."

"I apologize for my . . . tone. I meant to convey that your son may need professional help. It has been a very long and frustrating day, Mrs. Kardos. I'm going to have you talk to Esther Conde, our school's child psychologist and social worker. I want you to go see her with Javier. We may need to come up with an IEP, an individual education plan, for Javier."

"What does that mean?" I asked.

"It means finding a way to educate Javier given who he is." The man clearly did not like me. He wouldn't even look at me when he answered my question. He read through Javier's file. "I see that he has twelve unexcused absences. You, as a parent, are in violation of truancy laws. I can ask the juvenile justice system to get involved."

"Juvenile system," Julia repeated, her voice trembling.

"It doesn't have to be that way," Mr. Mallard said apologetically, possibly in response to the furious look on my face. How dare he threaten Julia! I was ready to pounce on him, and they could put *me* in jail for all I cared. "Look, all I'm saying is that this is a serious situation. We must do what is best for Javier and the safety of his classmates. Talk to Esther Conde. Let's come up with a plan."

"A plan for an emotionally disturbed kid," I said, with sarcasm.

"Again, I apologize for my words. Javier is . . . he needs guidance. That's what I meant to say."

"He has guidance at home," Julia said, hurt. "We try to take care of him."

There was a knock on one of the glass windows. One of the two women who were outside, the older of the two, was pointing at her watch. Mr. Mallard stood and said, "I'm sorry, I have a school committee meeting in half an hour."

Julia reached for the card that Mr. Mallard had slid across his desk and handed it to me. I put it in my wallet. "Thank you," Julia said meekly.

"You didn't have to thank him," I said to Julia when were out on the street. "The dude's a jerk. He couldn't even get your name right. I'd like to beat the emotionally disturbed crap outta him!" Julia did not hear a word I said. I could tell that her mind was on Javier. I wrapped the wool scarf around her neck and pulled down her hat so that her ears were covered. She started coughing again and I took out my phone to call an Uber.

"Those are expensive," Julia protested.

"I got money," I said.

When we got home from our visit with Mallard the Jerk, we found Javier asleep on the sofa. The long, unkempt hair made him look older than his twelve years, but he was still a good-looking kid, with Julia's caramel skin and delicate features. On the coffee table there lay one of the baggies with weed cigarettes that I sold at the fish market. Each bag contained twenty cigarettes that I roll myself. The people who buy them will pay an extra ten bucks for the weed when it's rolled up and ready to smoke. I counted the cigarettes left in the bag and saw that Javier had smoked four.

Julia shouted at me. "Get that junk out of the house! It's the reason Javier's the way he is!"

I didn't say anything. I knew she wasn't angry at me. She was angry at her lungs, at Mr. Mallard, at Javier's father, at this apartment, at the world. She should have been angry at Javier as well, but I knew that was hard for her. I went to the kitchen, got a glass of cold water, and splashed it on Javier's face.

"What you doing? Let him sleep," Julia shouted, but not too strongly. "I'll talk to him tomorrow."

"You need to talk to him now. Not tomorrow. Do you want him to turn into a criminal?"

Javier bolted up, water dripping from his face. "What the . . ."

I brought two chairs from the kitchen table and placed them in front of the sofa. Julia got my message and sat down. I did as well.

"What?" Javier looked at me and then at Julia. I studied his eyes. His black pupils were the size of cherries. My first impulse was to stand him up and search his pockets to see if he had any other drugs, but I decided to do that later, when

Julia wasn't looking. I didn't want to add to Julia's worries. Not today, anyway.

I looked at Julia, urging her to speak with the force of my eyes. Her voice was soft, kind, apologetic—the opposite, I thought, of the tone she should use with Javier. "Javier, mijo, why are you doing this? Hitting people at school. Smoking. We met with your principal this afternoon." Here Julia broke into a prolonged coughing fit. I got the glass I had used to splash water on Javier's face and filled it with water from a jar we kept in the fridge. All through Julia's coughing, Javier closed his eyes and grinned as if watching a movie inside his head. It took all that I had not to slap him. Finally, Julia was able to continue. "They want to send you to another school. One for kids who are emotionally . . ." Julia looked at me for help in finding the right word.

"Not able to follow rules," I said. I did not say the first thing that came to mind. I wanted to make sure I understood exactly what "emotionally disturbed" meant before I applied it to Javier.

"Like you?" Javier said, glancing at the bag of weed on the coffee table. His question surprised me. I didn't think he was awake enough to listen to what Julia was saying.

Julia gave me a quick, accusatory glance and continued, "We need to take you to see a social worker so you can stay in school."

Javier shrugged. "Can I go to sleep now?" He stood up, but I pushed him down gently. "We're not finished talking to you."

"You ain't my father!" Javier had a killer glare that would scare a grown man. I was used to it, but it still got my adrenaline going.

"But she's your mother and you better show some respect!" I gave Javier my own bring-it-on look. The last time I hit Javier was when he was eight. During one of his anger tantrums, when I was trying to control him, he kicked me in an extremely vulnerable place and I instinctively swung at his face and cracked his right eye socket. It was a mess. I made a promise to myself that I would never hit him again—an extremely hard promise to keep.

"Javi," Julia said, softly, "Qué vamos a hacer contigo?"

"What happened to the kid in school?" I asked, when Javier did not answer. I took deep breath and trying to control myself. "Why you hit him?"

"Wasn't no him. This Dominican bitch said . . ." Javier glanced at Julia and stopped.

"You hit a girl?" I asked, dismayed.

"She said my mother was a puta," Javier snapped.

Julia moved over to the sofa, put her arms around Javier.

"You shouldn't hit girls," was all I could think of saying. But part of me was proud he had defended our mother.

"Javi, who cares what people say," Julia said, lovingly.

Javier pulled himself slowly away from Julia's arms. In the space between the thumb and the index finger I saw a blue dot the size of a pin's head. The X-Tecas tattoo their hands with five dots forming a circle. One dot is an indication that you're starting on the road to eventually earn the five dots and the circle of a soldado. Violence against enemies of the X-Tecas is how an X-Teca earns the dots. Or you could kill someone and get an immediate circle.

I asked: "Did the X-Tecas do that?"

"What is that? Did you do that with a pen? You could get infected," Julia said, grabbing Javier's hand.

Javier pulled his hand away from Julia and stood. Then he looked at me. "Primo did it. He did it so everyone know I'll be blood. Soon." He moved past me and walked to his room. Julia and I were looking at each other, dumbfounded, when we heard the door slam.

"I'm so tired," Julia said, closing her eyes. "My chest hurts.

The coughing. There's some honey in a bear." She pointed to the counter next to the sink. "Can you get me some in a cup with a little hot water?"

"Want a sandwich or something? I can make you some soup."

"No, no. But you should have something. I didn't get a chance to cook anything. Javier should have some food too. I'll just close my eyes for a few minutes and then make you guys some arroz con pollo."

When I came back to the sofa, Julia was lying on her side, her head on a pink crocheted cushion. I put the cup of honey and water on the coffee table and was about to walk out when I looked at her again and let the sight really sink into me.

"Hey, you know, you've had that cough for a long time now. You've lost weight. You need to see a doctor."

She made room on the sofa and I sat with her.

"I will. I will. But listen to me. I want to tell you something. Javier's right; you're not his father and you shouldn't have to take care of him. That was Fernando's job. Only he said no."

"Really? That guy? Javier's better off with the X-Tecas."

Julia chuckled and then started to cough. I sat her up and fed her a spoon of honey. When she was calm again, she said,

"We have to try. There's some decency in Fernando, deep down, I know it. I want to take Javier to Doña Hortensia. She can put her blessings on him. Drive out the espíritu malo he carries inside. She can give me a little blessing también to get rid of this cough, this . . . I'm so tired I can barely walk. And you—maybe she can do something to open your eyes so you see the right girl when she stands in front of you." Julia winked at me and then closed her eyes, as if to let me know that my response was neither needed nor wanted.

I walked to Javier's room to check on him. He was asleep on his bed, fully clothed. I took off his sneakers and then I looked through his pockets. In the right-hand pocket, I found three tickets from Zobo's, a video arcade on Lafayette Avenue. In the left pocket, I found a white pill that I did not recognize. I knew what amphetamine pills looked like because Primo had been pushing me to sell those pills to the truckers who used them to pump up their metabolism so they could stay awake on long hauls. This pill was probably a kind of stimulant I had not seen before. I only hoped that Javier was selling the pills and not using them, but the size of his pupils when I first woke him up indicated to me that my hopes were unfounded. He had probably smoked the marijuana cigarettes to bring himself down from the jittery effect of the speed. I had seen the twitches and trembling hands of the truckers and did not want to imagine the effect of those pills on a twelve-year-old brain.

I spent another half hour searching Javier's room for pills or other drugs but didn't find anything. What I did find was a pop-up switchblade. I confiscated the switchblade. I didn't want Javier to use it on me.

Wednesday, February 8

I was coming out of school when I got the text from Julia. She was at BronxCare's ER. Her supervisor at Lux Linen sent her there when her coughing wouldn't stop. When I got to BronxCare, a nurse told me that Julia had been taken to radiology for a CT scan.

I had my laptop with me so I looked up *CT scan*. It is a more powerful, multidimensional X-ray used to get the exact location, size, and type of the "abnormalities" that may have shown up in a regular X-ray. I immediately began to think the worst. And the worst, I am sorry to say, included things like, what if Julia can't work at Lux Linen anymore? All the cleaning chemicals they use can't be good for her. And worse, if something happened to Julia, I would be stuck with Javier.

Fortunately, these dark thoughts went "poof" when I looked up and saw the girl who sat across from me. I thought Rosario had come back to life. The sudden shock of the apparition sent my laptop sprawling to the ground. "I didn't mean to scare you," the young woman said when I had finally managed to pull myself together. I looked at her again. The resemblance was not as close as my first impression. Her black hair, pulled back tightly into a ponytail, was different from Rosario's short auburn hair. Her eyes did not have the striking depth of Rosario's. Still, the young woman had a beauty that resembled Rosario's. "Is something wrong?" she asked, touching her face.

I realized I was staring. "No, no. You look like someone I know," I said, embarrassed.

I must have continued to stare at her because she said, "People tell me I remind them of someone else all the time. I must have a very common face."

"I don't think 'common' is how I would describe your face." I didn't mean to sound flirty.

"No?"

I reached for my phone and found the picture of Rosario

I took the day we walked to Barretto Point. I got up, sat on the chair next to the girl, and gave her my phone. She took it and studied the picture carefully. Rosario stood with her arms crossed, the East River in the background. I had tried to get her to smile, but all I got was a shy grin. She didn't like to have her picture taken and it showed.

"You think I look like her?" the young woman said, still looking at the picture.

"You don't think so?"

"No. Not really. She looks sad. I'm pretty much a happy person."

"She wasn't sad," I said defensively. "She was . . . thoughtful . . . that day." I took the phone back. I fully expected the girl to leave, but she stayed sitting next to me, her laptop still closed.

"I didn't mean to offend. Is she your girlfriend?"

"No. Just a friend."

"I'm Sabrina, by the way."

"Nico." I extended my hand. She looked at it for a few seconds as if wondering if it was okay to shake hands with someone in a hospital. When she finally took it, I said, "Nicolás Kardos, but people call me Nico."

"Sabrina Mendoza, but people call me Sabrina."

I giggled like an eighth grader at his first dance. All my usual suaveness had suddenly abandoned me. "You waiting for someone?" I looked in the direction of the double doors that led to the examining rooms.

"I'm waiting for my dad. He's on the hospital's board of directors. He's here to see some new technology the hospital acquired." She looked at the laptop open on my lap. "Schoolwork?"

"No, a . . . novel. I'm writing one." Why I felt the need to impress that girl at that moment, I have no idea.

"Wow! You're a writer?"

"Yes, going to be." I still can't believe I said that. I needed to change the subject quickly. "Where do you go to school?"

"Bronx Science." The way she said it—like she didn't want to brag.

"Oh. You must be smart."

"I am."

I nodded, hoping that the conversation was over. The girl had a snobbishness about her and, well, who needs that? I started to open my laptop when she asked, "What school do *you* go to?"

"Stonebridge Charter."

"That's in Hunts Point, isn't it?" Her facial expression was somewhere between disgusted and terrified.

"Yup. They got schools there, believe it or not." At that point, I didn't care if I sounded irritated.

"I'm sorry," she said, turning red. "I didn't mean that to come out the way it did."

"That's okay. I'm kind of prickly right now. Things, you know." I looked in the direction of the double doors. "I better go over to radiology and see how my mom's doing."

"Okay," she said.

I got up to leave. "Nice meeting you."

I had already taken a few steps toward the hallway that led to the back of the hospital when I heard her speak. "Nico, wait." She was standing behind me, holding her phone. "Let me see your phone. I'll AirDrop you my number. My mom knows lots of people in the publishing business. She can help with your novel. Call me."

I took my phone out.

A current of electricity went through me when I saw Rosario's smile on her face.

Thursday, February 9

They kept Julia overnight so they could do some tests. Today, after school, I went to see her. My mother was in a space enclosed by heavy white curtains. She was sitting on a bed that had been raised, wearing one of those paper nightgowns that opened in the back. A tiny bald man with the thickest black eyebrows I've ever seen shook my hand and said, "Nico, right?"

"Yes."

"I'm Jerry Zimmerman. I'll be looking after your mother. She tells me you're almost eighteen."

I nodded. Julia had her eyes averted from me, but I could see that she'd been crying. "How is she?"

Dr. Zimmerman cleared his throat. The way he did it, I could tell he was searching for the right words. Julia tried to smooth the wrinkles in her nightgown. Her hands were trembling. "The CT scan revealed four tumors in your mother's left lung and two in the other. We'll do a needle biopsy on one of the tumors tomorrow. The biopsy will tell us more about the kind of cells that form it and will help us determine how to proceed."

"Tumors? What kind of tumors?" I imagined little black golf balls inside Julia.

"We'll know more tomorrow," he said. "After the biopsy and after we see the results of the other tests we did today. Regardless of the results of the biopsy, I'd like to keep your mother here for a few more days. She's got liquid in her lungs we'd like to drain." Just before stepping out, he turned to Julia and spoke in perfect Spanish. "Le voy a conseguir un cuarto. No se preocupe. Aquí la vamos a cuidar muy bien."

I took a few steps so I could stand by Julia. "He speaks Spanish" was all I could think of saying.

"I was going to stop at the supermarket yesterday after we left here," Julia said. "We got nothing to eat but a can of SPAM. Maybe you can get a frozen dinner for you and Javier at the bodega. He likes the lasagna ones. Make sure you get the large one."

"Don't worry. We'll be okay." I lowered her bed and covered her with the thin hospital blanket. She was shivering so I went outside and grabbed two more blankets from a cart.

When I finished covering her, Julia held me by the wrist and spoke rapidly and with determination and firmness. "On Monday, that's when Doña Hortensia does healings. You'll have to skip school, I want you to take Javier to Doña Hortensia, and after she blesses him, I want you to tell her all that you heard from the doctor, about the tumors, about the cough, and then you come back and tell me what she said."

"Why?"

"Because she'll tell you the truth and I need to know the truth. I don't wanna no chemo and stuff if is no use. Doña Hortensia will advise me—"

I interrupted: "What are you talking about? You're jumping to all kinds of conclusions when you don't even know . . ."

Julia squeezed my wrist so hard that it hurt. "I'm asking you to do this for me. I'm not going to ask you again."

"All right, all right." She let go of my wrist and I rubbed it with my right hand. "I'll probably have to tie Javier to get him there, but I'll take him." Julia didn't smile as I had hoped.

She pointed to a blue plastic bedpan on the table next to the bed. "You need to pee? I can walk you to the bathroom." She shook her head and pointed to the bedpan again. I gave it to her and she motioned with flicking fingers for me to step outside. When I came back, she was holding a container filled with dark yellow liquid.

"Give this to Doña Hortensia," she instructed.

"She's not a doctor, Mami," I said, taking the container. Julia smiled. She seemed suddenly more relaxed.

"And when you're there, it wouldn't hurt you to tell her," Julia said enigmatically.

"Me? Tell her what?"

"I know you, Nico. You're more like me than you know. You been thinkin' about her all the time. I can tell. Your Rosario. Talk to Mrs. Hortensia 'bout her. Ask her to heal you. How she's still hurting inside you."

Julia, my mother. She spent her days washing and folding hotel sheets and pillowcases, but she had a way of seeing into the heart. "You're the only one could make her laugh," I said. "Remember?"

"She made me laugh too," Julia said, with sadness. I waited for Julia to smile and then I bent down and kissed her forehead.

Alma was waiting for me in my apartment. She and Pepito were sitting on the sofa watching cartoons. Alma looked up to see me and then down to the container of urine in my hand.

"It's Julia's," I said to her.

Friday, February 10, 2:40 a.m.

Finished Ruth's novel. Man, I feel as if there's no way I could ever write like that. Why even try? What a crappy feeling. It's as if Ruth has tools to reach a place I didn't even know existed. She was given a hammer and chisel to break through to a place of beauty she saw clearly. Where does beauty come from? For there is such a thing as beauty. I can't describe it. I can only imagine it exists. Ruth found it in her writing. Rosario did too.

It's so clear and simple, almost unnoticeable, the beauty that their words reveal. It is hidden yet obvious. It almost hurts, this beauty.

Where did Ruth and Rosario find it?

Sunday, February 12

S kipped writing in here yesterday. Hard to write after reading Ruth's novel.

Early this morning there was knocking on the door to our apartment. I could hear Noah and Alma on the other side, shouting at me to hurry and open the door. I looked at the digital clock next to my bed. It was eight. My head was spinning. My vision was blurry. I put a pair of blue jeans on and wobbled to the door. As soon as I opened it, Noah grabbed one hand and Alma the other. They began to drag me down the stairs.

"Let me get my jacket," I pleaded. I had on an old, plaid flannel shirt I liked to sleep with in the winter.

"Cold air is good for hangovers," Noah said. How the hell did he know I had drunk half a bottle of tequila last night? "You called me at two a.m. remember?"

I looked at Alma. "You called me at eleven," she said, answering my silent question.

I remembered I started drinking when Javier went to his room at nine and I vaguely recalled calling Alma. It was about Rosario, but about what exactly, I did not know. I had no recollection whatsoever of calling Noah.

Noah opened the doors to our building and pointed to a white pickup truck. It had the picture of a smiling orange fish and on the side of the fish the words SANTINI AND SON FISH WHOLESALER.

"Why's your dad's old truck here?" I said.

"The old man wants you to keep it so you can make some special deliveries and pickups and so you can get to work on time in the morning. Let's go get some practice runs."

"You realize I've been driving this truck for two years now."

"Driving it around the fish market's not the same. Have you ever parallel parked?" Noah whacked me on the back.

"I know a good place to practice." Alma grabbed the key from my hand and ran to the truck. She got in the driver's seat and I sat in between her and Noah. Alma made a

91

U-turn and then a right turn onto Lafayette Avenue.

"Where did you learn how to drive?" I asked, amazed. She drove like she'd been doing it for years.

"Ruben lets me drive his Caddy."

"No wonder," Noah said.

"No wonder what?" Alma protested.

"No wonder you drive like cops are chasing you."

I laughed and fist-bumped Noah.

"You guys are hilarious," Alma said.

"Where we going?" I asked.

"To the food co-op, the big parking lot for the trucks," Alma responded, distracted.

I felt a pang in my chest. Rosario worked at a place called Lushy Foods located at the food co-op.

"Only it's Sunday so no trucks," Noah added. Then, to me, "So, what's the next step with your mom?"

"They're doing more tests," I answered distractedly. I was thinking about how much Rosario hated working at Lushy Foods.

"Earth to Nico," Alma was saying.

When we got to the parking lot, Alma stopped the truck, went around to the other side, and I scooted over to the driver's seat. I drove around the lot and in between parked trucks for about twenty minutes with both Alma and Noah giving me directions. "Check the mirror before you change lanes. Blinkers. Don't forget the blinkers." They even made me parallel park into a space they created with empty beer bottles. After three unsuccessful tries, Noah told me to stop the truck and turn off the motor. Alma and Noah looked at each other like they didn't know who should go first.

"Oh, no way," I said, figuring out what was going on. "Is this like some kind of intervention or something?"

Alma jumped right in—she couldn't hold it in any longer. "What gives with the drinking? The last time you got drunk was at Rosario's funeral and you promised you'd never get drunk again. I know it's stressful with your mom right now, but . . ."

"What is it with you guys?" I said angrily. "It was one time! It's not like I do it every day. Or every other day." Here I looked directly at Noah.

"The addiction starts small," Noah said. His tone was of one speaking from experience. "You don't want to start down that road. Trust me. All we want to do is nip it in the butt."

"Bud," Alma corrected him. "It's bud, not butt."

"You of all people should not be preaching to me about alcohol," I said to Noah.

"Wrongo. Me of all people's the one to do it!" Noah's face turned red. He rolled down the window and started to take out a cigarette.

"Don't even think about it," Alma told him. Noah reluctantly put the pack back in his shirt pocket. Then Alma reached down for the ignition and started the truck. "It's freezing in here." Noah rolled up his window, but not all the way up. I thought they were done with me, but I was wrong.

"What exactly's bugging you?" Alma looked at me and then at Noah. They had some kind of secret agreement between them, I could tell.

"Yeah, what's up with all the questions about Rosario?" Noah asked.

I made a surprised face. "Rosario?"

"Last night you wanted to know about Rosario's laptop," Alma said. "I already told you I don't have it. It was lost."

"I did? I called you about that?"

"Yes."

There was a hurt look on both Noah's and Alma's faces. Maybe the hurt was the same. I was bringing up pain they wanted to leave behind.

"I'm sorry. I was reading something that reminded me

of Rosario. Her writing. I just . . . that laptop was where she kept her book of short stories, her journal, everything. She lived in that thing. Where could it have gone?"

"We don't know," Noah said. "Lots of things she did we don't know. Don't let it get to you."

I didn't tell them that what sent me to the bottle the night before was the realization that Ruth's novel was like the one and only short story that Rosario let me read. I mean, the subject matter was totally different. Ruth wrote fantasy and Rosario wrote about a nurse who worked with the elderly, but they both had something indescribable, something real that was hard to name. A brilliance of some sort that let me see something I had never seen before. Not so much see but recognize. A beauty I knew was there but was never able to grasp.

Also there was a warmth in their writing, as if the author was a friend who had felt what I had felt. I thought I was the only one, and knowing there was someone else made me less lonely. It wasn't just that I couldn't put their work down or that the characters were both like people I'd never met before but also people I always knew. It was the words they used and the way they joined them to make sentences that made me want to read them again just to make sure they were as beautiful as they seemed. And they were.

Their words were like diamonds and rubies and emeralds meticulously arranged in a dazzling necklace. I read some of what I had written in this journal and my writing seemed so poor. Poor. That's the best word for what came out from me. I was Hunts Point, and Rosario and Ruth were Park Avenue.

How could I possibly ever write with that kind of imagination and precision? It was impossible. I felt as if a tiny tube of dynamite had blasted open my forehead and I saw that the whole idea of being a writer was one big, jumbo-size delusion. It was no different than if I had suddenly gotten it into my head that I could play basketball for the Brooklyn Nets. I don't know what I was thinking. But whatever it was, it went poof, right there and then. I told myself just before the tequila took full effect that I was done thinking of this journal as a great piece of art, as a vehicle to fame and fortune. Finito with the illusions. If I kept writing, it was only because not doing it felt even worse.

"Okay," I said. "I got the message." I rubbed my temples. The tequila was also messaging me. "I'm hurting here."

I drove the three of us to a small Mexican restaurant on Oak Point Avenue. We each had a bowl of menudo and some tamales. I dropped Noah off at his apartment building and then I drove home with Alma. I was hoping she wouldn't bring up any serious topics, but my hope was unfounded.

"You never told me what happened with Primo. Ruben told me you talked to him."

"Let me find a parking spot first. I can't talk and park at the same time."

"There's one!"

"It's too tight."

"You're kidding! A school bus would fit in there."

I found a space a block away. I left the engine running so we could keep warm. I turned sideways to face Alma. "Primo wants me to find drivers who will sell stuff for him in Manhattan and Brooklyn."

"Wait, you're not . . . ?"

"I've been thinking it's not a bad offer. Primo said he'll do what he can to protect Javier, and with Julia getting sick . . ."

"You serious?"

"All I gotta do is find some delivery guys who come to pick up fish and then I will be the intermediary between them and the X-Tecas. Just coke and molly."

"Just coke and molly. Are you hearing yourself?

"Is it so bad?" Because it didn't seem all that bad to me.

"I can't believe this is happening again."

"Again?"

"People don't jump off cliffs, you know. They slide down slowly with tiny steps."

"Are you talking about Rosario? What is it that you're not telling me? The other day I found out from Noah that her last phone call was to Mr. Cortazar. A little detail you never bothered to tell me. Now this tiny step thing. Tell me."

"All I can tell you is that if you mess with the X-Tecas you'll be screwing up your life."

I looked at Alma long and hard. "Because that's very different from you going out with the second-in-command of the X-Tecas. I will never get it. I'm befuddled."

Alma turned to look at the falling snow. Small flakes floating gently down to earth. "Befuddled?" she said to herself.

"I'm trying out some new words. Okay, let's save this discussion for another day. I lost too many brain cells last night. I do have a favor to ask you," I said after a few minutes had gone by. "Javier really looks up to you—you being Ruben's woman and all." Alma gave me one of her killer looks. "Anyway, Julia wants me to take Javier to Doña Hortensia for a blessing and I also need to ask Doña Hortensia about Julia."

"Mexicans," Alma said, not unkindly.

"Yeah. So. Anyway. If you said a few words to Javier about how he needs to come with me."

"What if Ruben calls him and orders him to do whatever you say, go wherever you want him to go. That would be better, no?"

I wasn't sure whether there was an undercurrent of hostility in Alma's tone. Her eyes said that there wasn't. Her eyes said she cared for me and was worried about me, so I went with what her eyes were telling me. I didn't like the idea of Ruben helping me control Javier. It seemed cowardly and weak on my part. But I was tired, and my head hurt, and I felt like crap.

"Thank you," I said. "That would be helpful."

"When are you going to this curandera or bruja or whatever she is?"

"I was thinking of skipping school tomorrow. Going early, around nine, and then Javier and I can go see Julia at the hospital."

"Ruben will call Javier on your phone before then, okay?"

We walked back to our building. Alma stuck her tongue out to receive the snowflakes. She reminded me just then of the little girl I grew up with. Alma and me twirling a rope while Rosario jumped and sang in Spanish:

tin marín

de don pingue

cucara macara

titere fue

yo no fui

fue tete.

pégale a ella

que ella fue

Monday, February 13, 2:00 a.m.

I've been thinking all day that beauty is not something you have before you start writing. It's more like a thing you search for, desperately, in the act of writing.

Monday, February 13, 9:00 p.m.

I don't know what Ruben said to Javier, but he was like a different kid as I drove over to Doña Hortensia. The woman lived all the way in the South Bronx and the fastest way to get there was the Bruckner, but there was no way I was getting on that monster. I chose the longest route on the GPS and drove slowly. At home, after Ruben called, Javier went into his room and put on a white shirt and a pair of gray corduroy pants. His abundant black hair stayed in place thanks to a bottle of hairspray for men that Harrison had left in our bathroom. What was even stranger was that he didn't even ask who Doña Hortensia was or why we were going to see her. About ten minutes after we started off, he asked me if the truck was mine and I said that I wasn't sure that it was mine, as in that I was the new owner, but I thought we could keep it as long as we needed it.

"If you die, then it goes back to Noah?"

His words jolted me. For a moment there I thought he knew about my dream. I couldn't turn to look at him just then because I was trying to make a left on a busy intersection. "What makes you say that? You thinking of killing me?" I tried to joke.

"Things happen," he said, cool as a cucumber. It wasn't that Javier knew about my dream, I realized. He was just being a Hunts Point kid aware that brothers can die. Then he added, "Primo said you might help him out with some business. What business?"

"Look," I said, slowing down so I could talk and drive at the same time. "This thing with Mami could be serious. What if she's not be able to work? We can't make it any worse for her by what we do. You understand?"

"I'm not gonna live with my father if she dies."

"No one is saying anything about dying. Or about your father. But I may need to talk to the son of a bitch. He needs to pay up for the child support he owes Julia."

"I'll go with you. If he doesn't pay up, I'll kill him."

I sighed. "Why are you so full of violence? You're going to end up in juvie before you're fifteen." A green Toyota Corolla started honking behind us. We were going too slow. Javier rolled down the window and yelled a series of obscenities at them, some of which I had not heard in the combinations that Javier uttered them. I almost felt proud of him. This was my fearless little brother. The Toyota pulled up on my side and one of the men pointed what looked like a toy machine gun at me. A car coming in the opposite direction began to honk and the Toyota veered in front of me and sped away.

"Was that a real gun?" I asked, shaken.

"That was a KWC Mini Uzi. Nice, huh? Those pendejos were MS-13."

"How you know that?"

"There was a little blue-and-white flag on their antenna."

"You saw that flag when you looked back to see who was honking at us and you still decided to stick your head out the window and curse them? You could have gotten us killed, you know that?"

"Nah. There's too much traffic and they were showing their colors. MS-13s don't like attention. Not like the DDPs. Those putos, all they do is show off."

It dawned on me. "That Dominican girl you hit at school, she DDP?"

"Yup. Or wannabe. She knew I was X-Teca so she came after me. She was showing off."

We were at a stoplight, only a couple of blocks from Doña Hortensia's house. "Are you X-Teca?" I grabbed his left hand and turned it so I could look at the blue dot to see if another had joined it.

"I haven't been jumped-in yet," Javier said, pulling his hand away from me. "Primo wants me to wait." He looked at me, anger in his eyes. "It's gonna happen, I don't care what you or Alma say to Ruben. Primo's boss. He told me already that I'll be X-Teca, for sure. I need to be patient. That's why he gave me this first ink, so I knew, no doubt. I be full blood soon."

There in that truck, waiting for the light to turn green, it struck me for the first time that I could just wash my hands of Javier, let his miserable life take its course and he'd probably be dead in a couple of years. I wasn't his father, as both Javier and Julia had pointed out. He wasn't even a full brother, only half, so what exactly did I owe him? Nada.

Doña Hortensia lived in an actual house. It was an old wood house with peeling red paint, a cement path that led from the sidewalk to the steps of a bright green porch. The whole house looked like an old, sick parrot. Even though I had accompanied Julia to see Doña Hortensia a few times before, I was still amazed at the fact that houses existed in the Bronx and that a Mexican lived in one of them.

There was a sign on the front door that said, REMOVASE LOS ZAPATOS ANTES DE ENTRAR. LA PUERTA ESTÁ ABIERTA. Even with my poor Spanish, I knew "removase" was not correct. To my surprise, Javier started to removase the heavy work boots he was wearing. I did the same. I opened the door and let Javier go in first. Right away I saw a dozen or so shoes, men's, women's, and kids'. A smell of something like dead lilies and an oppressive heat hit us. Javier wrinkled his nose and gagged as if he were about to vomit. We dropped our shoes along with the rest, took off our jackets, and walked down the hall. To our right was a room filled with the owners of the shoes. All of them were sitting on aluminum folding chairs except for a couple of little kids who were playing on the floor with a broken fire truck. A few of the women had rosaries in their hands. Javier and I looked at each other with the same thought: *This is going to be a long, long wait.* I sighed. Javier cursed. There were chairs folded against a wooden staircase and I went to get a couple when a small, thin man with wispy white hair came down the stairs and said, "You go up now." The man was about Javier's size. I would have mistaken him for a young boy but for his hair and the wrinkles around his blue eyes. He walked around me and went inside a door behind the stairs.

"What he say?" Javier asked.

"He said to go up." I looked in the direction of the room full of people. "I'm not sure it's our turn."

"I ain't waitin' no four hours," Javier said on his way up.

A few steps from the top of the stairs there was a room with the door open. Doña Hortensia was sitting on a modern-looking rocking chair—the kind that slides back and forth rather than rock. She was wearing a gray polyester pantsuit with a purple blouse. Her hair was cut short like a boy's and white as a summer cloud. One of the walls in the room was lined with various saints. I recognized Saint Francis by the dove perched on his shoulder and Saint Martín de Porres, Julia's favorite, by his black skin. Behind Doña Hortensia was the famous portrait of Jesus reclining on a tree, arms open, welcoming the little children. A small cot with a Mexican serape was against one of the walls of the room and a massage table with purple sheets on another. Next to Doña Hortensia, there was a small bureau with a crucifix and a large bowl of water. The bowl of water reminded me that I had left Julia's urine sample in the truck.

"You're Julia's sons," Doña Hortensia said affectionately. How did she know that? Although I had come with Julia to her house, she had never seen me and certainly never seen Javier. I was about to say something when Doña Hortensia gestured for Javier to sit on one of the two wooden chairs in front of her. She looked at me with a beautiful smile and said, "I'll talk to this young man. Please close the door."

Doña Hortensia spoke English with a heavy Mexican accent and it took me a few seconds to realize she was asking me to leave. "I forgot something in the car. Julia wanted me to bring it to you. I'll be right back. I mean, I'll wait outside."

When I was at the bottom of the stairs the little man with the white hair motioned for me to follow him. I thought maybe he wanted me to go out the back of the house to not let all the waiting people know I had cut in front of them, but instead he asked me to sit down at the kitchen table, where a cup of café con leche was waiting for me. I took a sip of the coffee. It had a sweet cinnamon taste. The little man sat across from me and crossed his right leg over his left. He had these very tight black nylon socks that reminded me of my father. There was also a cup of the whitish coffee in front of him, but he didn't drink from it. He was looking at me with these beautiful aquamarine eyes and I had the sense that he knew all there was to know about me. I felt a soothing, loving warmth come over me and then the tears gushed out. At first, I tried to stop, embarrassed, but the little man was nodding and grinning as if urging me to open the gates and let the tears flow. What was I crying about? No anguished thoughts came to mind. I wasn't thinking of Rosario. The dream of being a great writer had gone poof, but that wasn't it either. I don't know why I was bawling like a baby other than it felt good to cry in front of the little man, who was sitting there watching me with eyes that were full of a kindness I had never felt coming from a man. He wasn't feeling sorry for me or being sentimental in any way. He was just there in a way that said he had felt what I was feeling but had made it through to a place where it didn't hurt as much, and I would too eventually. When I finally stopped, he gave me a napkin and I blew my nose.

"I don't know where that came from," I said.

The little man lifted his cup very daintily and took a sip. "My name is Benito Carstensen, but you can call me Benny." His voice was sweet, soft, feminine almost.

"Nico Kardos," I responded. "You're not going to believe this, but I never cry. I don't even remember the last time I cried."

"Oh, I believe it," he said, smiling. "Now, let's get down to business. You had some questions. Go ahead and ask them."

"Actually, I'm here because my mother wanted me to bring my brother to see Doña Hortensia and to give her, Doña Hortensia, some of her urine, my mother's. My mother's in the hospital. She thought Doña Hortensia could tell her . . . things . . . about how sick she was . . . the truth. She wanted to know the truth." The more I spoke, the harder it was to get the words out. It felt as if Benny already knew all that and he was waiting for me to tell him the real reason I was there. "I left the jar with the urine in the truck. I should go get it . . . so I have it for when Javier comes out. Javier, that's my brother, he's up there with Doña Hortensia."

"Yes, yes, sweetie, your brother is in good hands with my sister. She'll give him the answers to your mother's questions."

"But he . . ."

"He has all the information Hortensia needs. Hortensia, poor thing, takes on all terminal cases. It's a difficult job. I, on the other hand, I try to help those who can still be saved."

110

"Terminal?" I wasn't sure whether he was referring to my mother or to Javier.

"Oh, nothing is set in stone, of course. When I saw you and your brother a little while ago, I saw . . . well, I will tell you in a way that doesn't scare you. I saw two sets of probabilities. Let's just say one of you has a better chance of beating fate."

"Fate?"

"It's a word. I don't like it, but I don't have anything better. Fate, as in the cards you're dealt, as in where you're placed when you come into the world and what is given to you. Your reality, such as it is, including the traits of your character. Your mami—her fate is sealed. Your brother . . . well, there's still a wiggle of hope. It's up to him. Same goes for you. Nothing's set. You can choose. Go ahead, honey, ask me your question. The one that pertains to you and not to your mother or your brother."

I immediately thought about my dream and, after hesitating for a few moments, I proceeded to tell it to him. He listened, sometimes grinning, and sometimes covering his mouth as if to keep from gasping. When I tried to explain who Rosario was, he said he knew about her and urged me to continue. After I was done, he placed the palm of his hand over his heart and said, "That's so beautiful. What a gift of a dream! Didn't you feel it as a gift?"

"I wasn't scared," I said. "I felt . . ."

"Blessed?" Benny asked.

"I'm not religious," I said, glancing at a small wooden cross that hung from his neck on something that looked like a shoelace.

"Oh goodness, you don't need to be religious to feel blessed. Now, ask me your question."

"Rosario told me something . . . in the dream . . . I can't remember."

I was looking down at the floor. I don't know how much time passed before I looked up to see a smiling Benny. He was beaming with what I imagined could only be a kind of fatherly pride. "And that's your question? What Rosario said to you? Not whether the dream foretells your death or that of your mother and brother?"

"I . . . it didn't seem like I could do much about that part of the dream. But what Rosario said to me, her words . . ."

"Could help you?"

I'd never once thought I needed any kind of help, but Benny was right. Something opened inside me, and I saw a terrible loneliness. "Yes," I admitted. Both to Benny and to myself. "Help me."

"Oh, my Nico, my lovely Nico," Benny said, full of tenderness. "Rosario sent her message directly to your heart so you could discover it on your own. But I can tell you this: She didn't appear in your dream to make things worse for you. She came to help you, for sure."

"Help me?"

"To find your true work. To get on with it. That's all I can say, my baby. I'm so glad you came by today. It's not often I meet a soul who honors the world of spirit, like you do, with your dream." Benny squeezed my hands one more time and then hurried out of the kitchen. He stopped by the stairs and then came back to the doorway. Benny touched his heart and then went up the stairs.

Javier was outside, sitting on the top step of the porch. He had a pale, scared look. The cockiness he had walking in had vanished. I slapped him gently on the head and we walked to the truck. I wanted to get home as soon as possible and write down Benny's words. I kept repeating what he'd said to me so I wouldn't forget.

"Where we going?" Javier asked.

"To see Julia," I answered.

When we were a few blocks from the hospital, I asked Javier: "You okay? Anything I should know?"

"That woman was freaky wacko. She sprinkled my face with water out of a little bottle and it burned my eyes. Then . . ." Javier stopped.

"Then what?"

"She put her hand over my heart and . . ."

"And what?"

"Nothing. She had her eyes closed and was saying words I couldn't hear, like prayers."

Javier looked out the window.

A block went by before I asked: "Did she say anything to you?"

"What's a canica?"

"I think it's the Spanish word for *marble*. Why?"

"She said my heart was a canica of odio."

"Odio means . . ."

"I know what it means," Javier snapped.

We were at a stoplight, both of us watching a dog on the back of a truck. The dog was barking at us. Javier made a pistol with his thumb and index finger and proceeded to shoot the dog. I let the truck and dog pull away from us. "Did she say anything about how to get rid of this odio?"

Javier looked into my eyes and then quickly looked away. I had the distinct impression that Doña Hortensia had shown him a path toward dissolving hate and that path involved me.

We circled the block twice until I found a space big enough to pull in without parallel parking. Before we got out of the truck, I said, "Mami's going to ask you about your visit with Doña Hortensia. Do me a favor, tell her she helped you." Javier sat still. I could tell he wanted to say something else. "Go ahead. Say what you want to say."

"The woman back there said to choose . . ." Javier looked at me as if he had forgotten who I was and was now trying to remember.

"Choose what?"

"It was just a bunch of mierda. I'm not choosing you when the time comes. What time she talking about? After Mami dies I'm going to live with Primo."

The first thing that came to my mind was *Good riddance! Who the hell wants you? I'm not choosing you either.* Then, when the anger subsided, I asked, "After Mami dies? What exactly did Doña Hortensia say?"

Javier said, full of rage, "That pendeja woman said you should fix it so Mami's as comfortable as possible. That means Mami's a goner, right?"

Before I could answer, Javier opened the door to the truck and jumped out.

Tuesday, February 14

D r. Zimmerman was coming out of Julia's room when I got there this afternoon. He wanted Julia to stay in the hospital. How long? All he could say is "let's see what happens in a few days." When I went in, I was shocked to see how pale Julia was. Her cheek was clammy when I hugged her. Her breathing was shallow and her voice whispery. Julia's boyfriend, Harrison, was there looking like he wished he was anywhere else. He had brought Julia a dozen red roses for Valentine's Day.

Harrison went down to the cafeteria for a sandwich and Julia asked me to repeat all that Javier had told her about the visit with Doña Hortensia. When I gave her Doña Hortensia's message that I should fix it so she was comfortable as possible, she grew very quiet and then told me to ask Harrison to draw up papers so that her best friend, Alma's mother, could be Javier's and my guardian in case she died before I turned eighteen in April.

"After that you'll have to be Javier's guardian. There's no one else." Julia paused for a moment to let those words sink in. It was one of those moments where nothing but the naked truth would do. "It hurts more if we fool ourselves," Julia continued feverishly. "I need you. Get in touch with Lalo at work. Get my check for the last two weeks I worked there. Also, I got some sick leave coming to me. Talk to that counselor at Javier's school. We'll need money. Go see Fernando. He won't take Javier, but he'll come through with something if you push him. There's so much. I'm sorry, it all falls on you." Julia's determined look suddenly melted and she started to quietly sob.

"Come on, Mami," I said, "don't lose hope."

But my words sounded fake and hollow even to myself. Who was I to talk about hope to Julia? I had just been chained to a cinder block and dumped into the East River.

Wednesday, February 15, 2:36 a.m.

There's a darkness I can touch and taste. It starts in the gut and rises to the head like the black smoke of burning tires. Rosario must have entered this darkness around this time last year, maybe with tiny steps, like Alma says. Or is it the darkness that crawls into us? I saw it in you, Rosario, but did not know what it was. A light went out inside you. A dark wind powerful as truth blew out the spark of life and hope that had carried your days. I saw it clearly—the dimming in your eyes.

How long was it there, this *it doesn't matter anymore?* I did not see it. Me, whose life was paying attention to you. How come I didn't recognize it even the last time I saw you? Or is

119

it something we see in others and ignore because of what it could mean to us, what we would need to do?

Maybe I saw the *no longer give a damn* and did not know how deadly it was. Could be I had to experience *it* myself to see how you can hide it behind ordinary gestures. Is that it? I had to wait a year for my eyes to grow accustomed to the suffocating shadows.

Here it is now. Knocking. No, not knocking anymore. *It* came in and made itself at home. It's been wanting to enter since you left and now it is here. The dream of you opened the door. Benny said you came to help. My true work—to be with you. How else to interpret the *I no longer care* that's here.

It is what happened to you, Rosario, and I did not see it. I didn't. Well, I see it now.

Thursday, February 16

It was 9:30 a.m. when I woke up. I must have turned off the alarm clock when it went off at 3:30. I had missed work and school. I remembered that only a few days ago it bothered me to miss work or school. Now school, work, college, my bestseller journal, it all seemed like a rehearsal for a performance that was never going to happen. Things to do and places to go were for those who believed they'd live forever or for a long while at least. I walked over to the kitchen drawer where Julia kept the bills and I found the card for Esther Conde, MSW. I needed to keep moving. I could feel a kind of who-gives-a-crap paralysis already taking over. I forced myself to think of Julia. Julia was going, just like the dream predicted, but while she was here she deserved better than me turning into a slug. I walked over to Javier's room. I expected him to be sleeping, but to my surprise the room was empty. The orange school backpack was gone. The kid had done what I could not do—he had gotten himself out in the world.

I went back to my room and sat at my desk. I kept thinking about how easy it would be to walk down two blocks and buy something from the X-Tecas to make me feel good again, if only for a little while. It must have been like that for Rosario. You look for something to get you through the day.

I was suddenly out of breath. I got up and walked around the room. I went to the window and looked out. For some reason our building was slightly higher than the identical building next door and I could see Mrs. Reyes's small roof garden, the tomato plants now brown and withered. There was not enough air in the room.

I grabbed my phone, found the number I was looking for, and texted:

Hey, want to hang? I can meet you someplace.

I knew it was the kind of message that would never get a response, but it felt good to send it. She was my drug—the girl who looked like Rosario.

Since Sabrina was not around, my imagination turned to the bottle of tequila under the sink. I went over to check. There was not much left. I looked in the Quaker Oats box where Julia kept the grocery money. There was forty-two dollars in there. I hesitated only for a second. I really, really could use a little numbness right then. Tomorrow I'd go back to the grind. I grabbed a twenty-dollar bill and was getting ready to go to Palacio Wine and Spirits when I heard my phone ping. I had to sit down on my desk chair when I read the text message:

Good timing! I'm playing hooky today.
Like you? Entrance to the Bronx Zoo? Noon?

"Bingo!" I said out loud. My response to Sabrina was more mature:

Cool. See you then.

But I needed money I didn't have. I could borrow the money from Alma. I knew where she kept the money she earned from babysitting. There was no one at Alma's and I had a key to her apartment.

Alma's bed was made and everything in her room was orderly. On her bedstand there was a plastic globe of the world. Alma had a globe on her desk where she kept money from working at Cachitos Daycare—whatever was left over after she helped out with rent and food. I opened the globe (it came apart around the equator) and took out a hundred-dollar bill. There were three hundred-dollar bills inside the globe. I told myself that I would put the money back next week. I was about to close the globe when I saw a small business card among the bills. On one side was the name of a detective from the New York Police Department. On the other side was a note written in Alma's handwriting.

Call about Rosario's things.

I read the name on the card again: Joseph Delgado. Right at that moment, I felt a strong urge to take the card and call Joseph Delgado. It was almost as if Rosario was there whispering in my ear. I placed the card and the money in my wallet and left Alma's apartment.

I left around eleven. I found a space in the back of a church near the zoo. They were having some fundraising sale, so I thought it'd be safe to leave the truck there. I walked into the church to stay warm until noon rolled around. It was a clean, simple, poor church without any statutes of saints. The perfect place to ask myself what the hell I was doing. The energy I had while driving was too high voltage to contain, but it was slowing down enough for me to see that I really did not want to see this girl. I wasn't going to her for who she was. She was, what? A simulacrum of Rosario? I could leave. Only I couldn't. At quarter to twelve, I zipped up my coat and walked over to the main entrance of the zoo.

I checked my cell phone. It was ten after twelve. I sat on one of the cement cylinders supposed to keep a terrorist from driving up to the entrance and exploding car and self. I sat there and sat there and at twelve forty-five, I decided that Sabrina had somehow made the right decision for both of us. The decision I didn't have the guts to make. I started to walk back to the church when I heard my name called. "Nico! Nico!" I turned and there was Sabrina running toward me in her white goose-down parka, pink wool cap, and brown leather boots. "I'm so sorry I'm late."

"I just got here myself," I lied again. The girl was stunning. Stealing from Alma and lying to myself seemed a small price to pay to just be there at that moment standing within touching distance of this apparition. She was just what was needed. "Maybe we can get some coffee someplace."

"I know the perfect place," she said, hooking her arm through mine and making my heart turn a half dozen somersaults.

"Don't you want to go in?"

"I'm not really a zoo person. I just thought this be an easy place to meet."

"Wow," I said when I saw the white Mercedes blink its lights.

"It's my mother's," Sabrina said. "I borrowed it for the afternoon. Much better than my Prius. What do you drive?"

"A truck. A Ford Ranger. I need it for work. For my work at the fish market."

"Mmm. I like guys with trucks."

"Okay." I felt heat so I opened my coat.

In the console between the seats, there were two cups of Starbucks coffee and a white paper bag. "Have you eaten? I got us a couple of chicken-salad croissants. I thought it'd be easier to have lunch here and . . . talk. I know a great parking spot. You game?"

"Yeah, sure."

"You can adjust your own temperature. Do you like your bum warm or hot?"

"What?"

"The seats are heated. You can control the temperature here." Sabrina pointed at the control screen. I opted for no heat. Sabrina started the car and drove. At the next stoplight, both of us took off our coats. "I'm glad you texted me. It took you a while."

"Really?"

"Longer than I expected."

"Things have been happening."

"Your mom? How is she?"

"She's in the hospital. Tests." It seemed too much to play the pity card, so I didn't. It was my only noble moment that day.

"Oh, gosh. I hope she gets better. So, here we are. Fordham University. Isn't it beautiful? My mother teaches here." Sabrina pointed to a sticker on her side of the windshield. "I'm supposed to be in that building, studying."

"You're a student here? I thought you went to Bronx Science."

"I do. But I take a course here and I come here to study. I'm not really playing hooky. I have a lot of independent research courses." Sabrina turned into an alley between two buildings.

She found a spot and parked. She left the car running. "This is my mom's parking spot. She has an office on the second floor. You want to see it? It has a great view."

"The view is pretty good from here," I said, looking in her direction. "But yes, I'd like to see it."

Sabrina's mother's office had one of those expensive oriental rugs that my father imports from Turkey. All the walls were lined with bookcases bulging with books. Sabrina opened the white curtains and we stood side by side watching a medieval-looking tower straight out of Ruth Silvester's novel. "The University Church," Sabrina said. "I like to study here. It's inspiring. Come, let's sit and have some lunch. It's not much."

Sabrina sat on the dark brown leather sofa that took up almost a full wall of the room. I was going to sit on the chair in front of it, but Sabrina motioned for me to sit next to her. She gave me one of the croissant sandwiches and I began to unwrap it. "What does your mom teach?" I asked before taking a bite.

"English. She's the head of the department. Her specialty is American poetry. Whitman, Dickinson. Those guys."

"Wow."

Sabrina took a bite from her sandwich. She found a napkin and wiped the corner of her mouth. "My dad is totally left brain. He's a lawyer. He started his own firm right out of law school and now he has some thirty lawyers and twenty paralegals. They do all kinds of law, but my father is a litigator. If you ever want to sue anyone, he's your man."

"That's good to know." I thought of Fernando Rojas and Mr. Mallard.

"Mom wanted me to be a teacher and Papi wanted me to be a lawyer."

"So . . ."

"Papi won. I got REA'd into Stanford, early admission, but I'm an only child and Mami and Papi want me close. I would love to go to California, but I'm staying close for them. Columbia's okay. But listen to me, babbling on. What about you? Where are you headed in the fall?"

"Um." I quickly swallowed what I was chewing and then took a sip of cold coffee. "Sarah Lawrence. Fingers crossed. I'm waiting to hear. They got a great writing program so that's my first choice."

"And you're a writer. Tell me about your novel?"

"What?"

"Your novel. At the hospital, you told me you were writing a novel. Mami's gonna love you. Tell me about it."

I watched Sabrina's eyes light up and bathe me with a soft admiring glance. There was a current pushing me in the direction of lying. Was it so bad to jump into that glow of acceptance and soak in it for a while? What I was feeling just then was so much better than what I'd felt the night before and that morning. "It's a fantasy. Nothing very original. It's a poor imitation of Tolkien. It's even got elves in it." How the hell did this come out of my mouth? I swear that it was out before I knew it. Anyway, what could I say to this girl who seemed so surprisingly taken with me? I'm writing a journal of my sad and dreary days.

"No way! I love fantasy. I adore *Game of Thrones*. I didn't read the books, but the series was awesome! Can I read your novel? Please? Will you send it to me?"

"Sure, sure. I'm almost done touching it up a bit."

My phone began to ring with calls from Alma. I turned off the phone. Sabrina and I continued talking for another ten minutes or so. At some point she got up to throw away the sandwich wrappers and when she came back, she sat down so close to me I could feel sparks fly between us.

"I love the color of your skin," she said, touching my arm.

130

I didn't respond. Just then I was thinking about Rosario. I was twelve and she was thirteen and we were coming back from Osorio's bodega carrying snacks and sodas for Alma's birthday party. We were about to enter our building when Rosario stopped, dropped her bag, turned me toward her, and asked: "Have you ever kissed a girl?"

"Like a *real* girl?" I asked. It was a question I regretted for many days.

Rosario, with plastic bags hanging from her arms, leaned forward until her lips touched mine. I was too dazed to hear properly, but I think she said, "Now you have."

Now there I was lost in the memory of Rosario while kissing a girl who was beautiful but decidedly not Rosario. The kisses were skin-deep only. Rosario's tiny peck when I was twelve reached my soul and settled permanently in there. For a moment, I thought of gently pushing the girl away, but the kisses were soft, and I responded to them as if her lips were Rosario's.

But there came a point when, as Julia said, it hurts more if we fool ourselves. Gently, very gently, I pulled out of the embrace.

"Mami is out of town, don't worry. No one's going to come in." This was in response to me starting to get up.

"I . . . should be heading back." I tried not to sound too eager to leave.

"What's wrong?"

"Nothing. My head. It's not you."

"You know, once I start at Columbia, it'll be all study and very little fun. I won't have time for relationships."

"Got it," I said. "I feel the same way about my writing. I'm going to give it everything I got."

"We should take advantage of this time, no?"

"Yes. I think we should. For sure."

"My mother knows all the big agents in New York. She can help you. Send me your novel, okay?"

"I will. Word."

"I like you. I didn't expect this. You're kind of different. We can see each other again if you want. I'm traveling to Europe in August and after that school starts. But we'd have, let's see, April, May, June, and July, four months to hang out. You'd have to promise not to get serious."

"I promise." This time I wasn't lying. I slid out of her embrace. "I do have to get back. I could walk to my truck. It's a short walk."

"I'm not going to let you walk!" She climbed out of the sofa

132

and began to straighten her hair. On the way back to the truck, she said, "You seem sad. Are you all right?"

"I got so much on my mind right now. I'm sorry."

"It's okay."

"I parked behind that church. I'll text you tonight," I lied. I was tempted to thank her but decided against it. Then, as I opened the door of the car to get out, I had a powerful urge to turn around and confess all my lies and exaggerations. I did not yield to this urge. The chances of me seeing Sabrina Mendoza again were zero to none.

Friday, February 17

S kipped school again today. The whole Sabrina episode gave me a nausea at myself. Nico Kardos nausea, let's call it. It was in this state of self-disgust that I did what I did next. Even though I had once said no to Primo's proposal to deal drugs, it now felt like something I wanted to do. Had to do. That's the best explanation I have for why I went looking for drivers willing to sell for me. Yeah, me, about to become an independent contractor to the X-Tecas. I know this journal is where you tell the truth, dig up the hidden motives and all that. What made me start digging my grave, as it were? Because stepping on the X-Teca path will surely put me in that coffin, sooner if not later. Hey, they don't call the whole drug business self-destructive for nothing. But here's a strange thing. The two guys who agreed, who will sell the stuff for me, said they'll do it only because it's me they'd be working with. What I want to say is that I went out looking for people out of the dark, stinking glob of nastiness that's settled in me and I came out feeling good, respected. Go figure.

Alma was sitting on my sofa watching cartoons with Pepito when I got back. "Mami's selling cosmetics to the neighbors. There're eight of them in our apartment. Don't ask. Where you been all day? You skipped school again?"

"It's a long story. I'll tell you later." The last thing I wanted to tell Alma was that I had spent the day looking for drivers willing to sell cocaine.

Alma could tell I was lying, of course. But she didn't interrogate me, fortunately. "Your mom's been calling."

"She was okay last time I saw her," I said quickly and in a way that would hopefully cut off any further inquiries into my day. "What she say?"

"She said the doctor wanted to talk to you." I got my cell phone out and called Dr. Zimmerman. He wasn't in. I left a message.

Alma opened the door a crack and looked out. "Okay. I think they're gone." She grabbed Pepito by the hand and was almost out of the room when she asked without turning around, "Are you seeing someone?"

"No. Why do you ask?" I tried not to look guilty, but Alma has a look, a kind of scrunching of the eyebrows, that would make a saint feel guilty.

"You're up to something, I can tell." Just then Pepito ran down the hall. "Later." The way she said it—the interrogation was not over.

A few minutes later, Dr. Zimmerman called. His voice was unhurried, almost a whisper. "The shallow breathing is the result of fluid in the lungs. We're draining it every few hours, but it still builds up. The tumors on her lungs. The tests show they're malignant."

All I could think of at that moment were the two empty chairs in my dream. Then, *If I can only get rid of Javier.* My mind was crumbling, no doubt. I shook off the thoughts and asked what everyone asks: "How long?"

But Dr. Zimmerman refused to answer. "Let's concentrate on what we can do to prolong her life. There are still things we can do. I'll go over the options with your mom and you two can discuss, okay? Let's keep fighting."

Easy for you to say, I thought.

Later that night, I went over to Noah's. He was in his room sitting up in bed, a bottle of vodka by his side. I shook my head when I saw it.

"Please don't preach at me."

I pulled out a desk chair and sat down. Immediately, I felt it had been a mistake to come to his house. I wanted company after Dr. Zimmerman's call, but Noah was half-drunk and angry. "Hey," he said, loud. "You know how you were asking about Rosario the other day, about her phone call to Mr. Cortazar? And then you were asking Alma about her laptop?"

"Yeah?"

"Well, hell, knock it off! Stop it. No more about Rosario!" I laughed, thinking that Noah was joking, but the flash of anger in his eyes told me he wasn't. "She's not yours to keep thinking about!" Spittle came out of his mouth.

I stood, suddenly. "Are you serious?"

"Yeah, it's not right. Like your obsessing about her. I'm okay you having a crush on her and everything, but enough is enough. She's dead. Let her rest in peace."

"I never . . ."

"Stop! Just stop! And stop acting like her. Moping around like the world's ending. I thought maybe it was your mom, but it's not even that. You get this superior attitude like you're a writer feeling stuff rest of us can't. Like that. You think you're someplace us ordinary people can't go. Lock me up in damn freezer the other day! Rosario used to be around me like I wasn't there, like I was invisible, her mind busy with important things she didn't think I could understand. Okay, from her maybe that was true. But you're not like her. Not even close. She never even liked you, if you wanna know the truth. She was sick of you imitatin' her. Wannabe writer and all. So stop thinking about her! You got no right to feel the way you do."

"I don't . . ."

Noah stuck his hand out. He took a deep breath and then: "You can lie to me all you want, but don't lie to yourself." Noah's piercing, fierce look penetrated my insides like some kind of fiery X-ray. He saw everything that was there, all that existed in my heart for Rosario.

"I never meant to hurt you," I said, full of more remorse than I had felt in a very long time. I started to walk away.

"Hey." Noah's voice was softer now. "Either on purpose

or by accident, Rosario is dead. One way or another. Does it matter?"

"Yes," I said. "It does to me."

It was quite possibly the only truthful thing I had said or done in a long time.

Saturday, February 18

What does it matter whether you took your life or not, Rosario? Why does it matter to me?

Not sure I'm going to find the answer to that or anything else sitting here writing. It's like I keep moving my fingers even though someone cut the electrical wire that connected them to my brain. Like when you cut the head of a snake and the rest keeps wiggling. Not that I've ever seen that. Read it someplace. Does everything we do have to make sense all the time? I got two guys who work at fancy restaurants to sell cocaine and ecstasy for me and when I was talking to them I thought it was the stupidest thing to be doing ever and there I was sounding convincing and confident. I sounded like Primo.

I felt powerful. Thing is, Rosario, Noah maybe was right when he told me that I go around acting like you. Not on purpose, maybe, but yeah. I can't put my finger on it, but it feels as if you are asking me to follow you. Not just follow you to where you are but in the way you were, how you moved around this place as if you owned it and how you couldn't make it yours.

This place couldn't hold you. Where else could you go?

This writing is like going nowhere in circles. Why does it feel like I'm writing to somebody even when I know it's just me? Am I writing to you, Rosario? Are you reading this? The thread I'm holding on to is the one where you didn't take your life. Because. If you couldn't find a thread to guide your steps into living, then maybe there's none.

Sunday, February 19

The afternoon that Rosario and I walked to Barretto Point was early March, a year ago, four months before her death. It was one of those unusual early spring days when the temperature reached 60 degrees. I was coming home from school when I saw Rosario standing outside our building talking on her cell.

"Bad news?" I asked when I saw her frown.

"Nicolás, walk with me to Barretto Point. Noah just called. He can't make it. Something about an ice box that broke. I made a picnic."

"Barretto Point? That's a hike," I pretended to object. "Can we take an Uber?"

"It's a fifteen-minute walk." Rosario grabbed my arm and began to pull me.

"Wait. Let me drop off my books at least."

I flew up the stairs and tossed my backpack into our apartment. A walk with Rosario on the first semi-warm day of the year. I only wished that the fifteen-minute walk could have been two hours.

We had sandwiches on a bench overlooking the East River. We talked about the short stories she was writing. She was taking Mr. Cortazar's creative writing class. Her goal to have twelve short stories by her graduation in May—a book she hoped to publish—had almost been reached. She was revising and getting ready to send out to agents.

When there was a pause in the conversation, I said, "Noah is a different man since you two started going out." Rosario smiled and nodded. Then a look of sadness came over her eyes.

"What is it? You're not happy with Noah?" It's very possible that at that moment I wanted her answer to be no.

She stared for a long time at the river. Then, "What's happy feel like? You know?"

"This." I gestured at the day, the blue sky, a white cloud.

Rosario smiled and I'd like to think she understood that

"this" included her and me sitting on a bench talking. "Noah is a good man," she finally said. "I'm lucky."

"But?"

She shook her head. "Maybe there's something wrong with us, Nico. Maybe it's the wanting to be writers that makes us . . . dissatisfied. No matter what we have, we think there's something better out there. Why?"

"You're dissatisfied? With Noah?"

"I'm speaking generally. Universally. It's a hunger. And an arrogance. Admit it, you're that way too. Deep down we think we're better. We feel more. See more. We're unhappy more. Deep down there's this feeling that no one's like us. And the people who love us are not good enough. We end up taking their love for granted. Like, of course you love me, why wouldn't you? Do you feel that way?"

"No, not really."

"Nicolás. Be honest. You don't feel that way toward Alma? You know she loves you."

"Yeah. I love her too. She's like my sister."

"That's not how she loves you. You know that."

"It's not because she's not good enough. It's not because of that." I felt Rosario's hot gaze on me and all that I could do was look away. "What I feel for her or don't feel has nothing to do with me being an artist or a writer, as you say." I stopped. I wanted to tell her that my heart was taken, fully, completely. With her, Rosario. Instead, I said, "Hey, remember when you moved to our apartment building? Your mom parked the U-Haul across the street and you came out and handed me a bag to carry upstairs. You were bossy from the word go."

Rosario shook her head slowly, but the smile told me she remembered. "We are sick romantics. We prefer the mirage in our minds to the flesh and blood in front of us."

"That's not the case for me." I took my index finger and touched her flesh-and-blood forearm.

Rosario didn't smile like I hoped. "I'm just an idea in your head. Alma is the one who's real." There was sudden anger on her face, and I knew it was directed at me—at the person who hurt her sister. When she spoke again, the anger was subdued, but still there. "I like Noah. He keeps me grounded. He reminds me I'm ordinary. He doesn't see me as some special gifted being—like I see myself. I *need* him. We *need* the Noahs and Almas in our lives. You know?"

All I knew was what I felt for her was real. It is possible

that at that moment she knew exactly what I felt. It's possible that she did. After a while, she put her arm around my shoulder and leaned her head on mine. She whispered: "You're all right, Nicolás. We're quite a pair, aren't we? Come on, let's go home."

Monday, February 20

Ruth was coming out of the hospital just as I was going in. "What are you doing here?" I asked.

"Picking up some medicine. And you?"

I pointed to a couple of empty chairs. "You got a sec?" When we were seated, I said, "My mother. Her lungs. She's here for a while."

"Is it serious?" she asked.

"Yes." And then, before she could say anything else: "I read your novel."

"Oh . . . please. You don't have to talk about that now." Ruth looked up as if pointing to my mother's hospital room.

"I did read it. Before everything started to happen with my

mom. I don't know how to tell you this in a way that doesn't sound clichéish. Is that a word, clichéish?"

"I don't think so." Getting a smile out of Ruth was a rare and precious event.

"Your novel made me . . . it made me stop wanting to be a writer. I will never write anything as beautiful as that. Why even try?"

Ruth covered her mouth with the fingers of her hand. "Oh no."

"It's so perfect. The details. The language of the Iffors, the battles with the Rowenfros, it's all so real. Every single one of the characters is so interesting: King Vingur and Princess Eteria and the evil wizard, Dortar. It's not just the characters and the plot and the detailed description, but also the language. Each sentence is different; the words and how you combine them are captivating but also accurate. Clear. The words disappear and I'm there in Sefendor. I know it sounds like I'm exaggerating, but I'm not. I even lied and told someone I had written it."

Ruth listened to my words, eyes lowered and cheeks gradually going from pink to bright red. Finally, she looked into my eyes and said, "That's the nicest thing anyone has ever said to me. Ever."

"You don't believe me. You think I'm exaggerating or just being nice, afraid to hurt your feelings?"

"No, no. I believe you were being truthful. It's just that . . ." Here Ruth reached out and fiddled with an ugly black purse she was carrying. "You said my novel made you want to stop writing, but did it really?"

"I've kept on. But . . . it's different now."

"How?"

"I don't know. It's more of a search, I guess. Just trying to find a thread, to make sense of the days, you know."

"And before?"

"I started writing to be famous and make loads of money. I wanted to be admired and have beautiful girls fall immediately in love with me. It wouldn't hurt to have more than forty followers on social media. That was my motivation. And . . ."

"And?"

"Rosario. You know, the girl in my dream. I wanted to be a writer like her. She was in eighth grade and I was in seventh when she told me she was going to be a writer. A few months after that, me too. I started writing. Poems at first. It was a way to impress her . . . for her to like me."

Ruth smiled, grateful for the truth.

149

We were silent for a while and then a thought came to me. "Maybe I'm still trying to impress her."

Ruth kept her eyes softly on mine for the longest time. When she finally spoke, it was with a tone that mirrored my honesty. "You know what I did to write this novel? I read all the fantasy books I could get my hands on, especially the bestsellers. I studied them until I had the basic patterns and rules ingrained in me. I wrote and rewrote passages until the vocabulary and the rhythm became second nature. I learned how the characters in the most popular novels speak and I had mine speak the same way—even if I don't speak that way. After two years of studying, I mean studying like I study chemistry, I knew I could do it. I had the formula and I knew how to use it." Ruth paused for a moment. "My book is not the kind of honest writing that you're doing."

"Honest writing. You and Mr. Cortazar. Please tell me what that means."

"Like you said a little while ago. Writing to find a thread to make sense of the days. I guess I would add, sharing whatever you find, for their sake."

"I think you did that in your own way. You made something

beautiful. So what if you followed what others have done? You're not pretending to be original. That's a kind of honesty. You should be proud of your work. Why not put your name on it?"

"I'd love it if the book got published and made tons of money. I'd put the money to good use. But why is my name or who I am important? Maybe I need anonymity to make sure I am honest in my work." We looked at each other for a long time. Then she said, blushing, "I don't know why I feel I can say these things to you. You must think I'm weird."

"I don't know many people like you. Are you even on social media?" Ruth covered her mouth and laughed. "Seriously? You aren't, are you? I don't think you're sharing what you find as best you can. To use your own words."

Ruth lowered her head and just then she looked exactly the way she had looked in the dream. "Writing *Orchidea* was good, but . . ."

"But?"

"Writing is not what I'm meant to do. I know that now. I've been helping out at my parents' clinic for a couple of years now. I really like it. With *Orchidea* it was just a part of me, but with medicine it's all of me. Head, heart, soul. I'm good at it too. So I'm going to say yes to Cornell and enroll in their premed program. I'm really happy with that decision. Also, to tell you the truth, it will be good to get out of the city for a while. Cornell is in upstate New York, in Ithaca. It's a beautiful campus. Lots of trees."

"Wow! Maybe you can give me some of your creative juice since you're not gonna be needin' it anymore."

Ruth giggled and then stood. "I got to head back to the urgent care."

"You didn't go to school today?"

"It's Presidents' Day. Remember? Speaking of school, I haven't seen you around there much."

"Yeah, things."

"Nico . . ." Ruth hesitated, then said, "I've thought a lot about your dream since the other day. It felt . . . special. I felt privileged that you shared it with me. And now you read my novel with so much care. I . . . thank you. I want to thank you."

I almost told Ruth she was in my dream. Not only was she in my dream, but she was visibly sad for me, as if I meant something to her. I didn't tell her anything. I didn't tell her I thought we were meant to be friends. I should have told her, I wanted to, but I didn't. As I walked to the elevator, I felt the kind of loneliness you feel when you have a chance to be close to someone, but you choose to stay distant.

Tuesday, February 21

Javier woke me up this morning. He was holding my phone in his hand. Julia was on the line. Her voice was raspy and whispery. I could barely hear her.

"Are you still in bed? You okay? They just called from Javier's school. Go talk to that counselor. They gonna send social services if you don't . . ."

There was another woman's voice and then we were disconnected. I sat up. Tried to focus on Javier's blurry face. I cleared my throat. "Let me guess. You haven't been going to school?"

"What *you* been doin'?" Javier gave a slight kick to the empty bottle of tequila next to my bed.

154

"We're going to see this Conde woman so they don't send social services and they stop calling Julia and then you can do whatever." I grabbed my head with both hands to see if I could put it back together.

"Awright," Javier said with a grin. "Can we stop at McDonald's? There's no food around here."

Esther Conde was a small woman about the same size as and only a little heavier than Javier. She was reluctant to speak to Javier without my mother present until I explained to her the reasons why Julia couldn't come. I thought that, as a psychologist, she would want to talk to Javier alone, but she asked me to come into her office. Could be she was afraid of him. She was located at the opposite end of the hall from Mr. Mallard's office in a room that I'm sure once served as a janitor's closet. She sat behind a green army-like desk and read from a file identical to the one that Mr. Mallard had read from.

She closed the file and looked directly into Javier's eyes. "You're lucky the girl's parents aren't filing charges against you. Do you know how lucky you are?"

Javier glowered at her.

"Answer Ms. Conde," I said, elbowing him.

"Mrs.," Esther Conde corrected me.

"Stupid question. *Do you know how lucky you are?*" Javier imitated Mrs. Conde's nasal tone.

Mrs. Conde's cheeks turned crimson, but she received Javier's words with an imperturbable grin. "You could be charged with assault and end up in a juvenile detention center even if the girl's parents don't want to press charges."

"Go for it," Javier snarled.

"What are our options here?" I asked, trying to break the tension. I could see Javier's boiling point approaching and I didn't want to be there when it did. "Mr. Mallard talked about a plan. What do we need to do?"

"The fact that you're *finally* here is a good start; took you all long enough."

"Sorry. Like I said. My mother . . ."

"Sorry about that." Mrs. Conde said quickly and then turned to Javier. "I'd like to hear from you what's going to happen when you go back to school. Are you going to hit a classmate again? Or a teacher?"

"You know what's strange here?" I said when I saw that Javier had no intention of answering Mrs. Conde's questions. "No one has asked Javier to tell his side of the story."

"That's because the school has a zero tolerance on violence

policy. Javier hit someone. Not for the first time, apparently."
She glanced down at the closed file in front of her. "Well, what
are you going to do if you go back to school?" Mrs. Conde's
eyes bore down on Javier.

Javier turned to look at me. There was something rare in
his eyes, something like kindness. He wanted me to know
that the only reason he wasn't telling Mrs. Conde to go to
hell, or possibly jumping over the desk and pummeling her,
was because he didn't want to make my life harder. I also
understood that this was a temporary concession, like one of
those truces where armies stop fighting so they can pick up
their dead. I nodded that I understood the message he sent
and was grateful. Then Javier turned to Mrs. Conde and said,
"I ain't hittin' anyone unless I have to."

"Unless you have to?" Mrs. Conde asked.

"If someone comes at me, I'm gonna defend myself!"

Mrs. Conde shook her head.

"Come on," I said, irritated. Javier was trying. He was
there. She didn't know how lucky we were it only took two
Egg McMuffins to get him there. She should take what she
could get. "Let's be realistic here."

"Why are you so angry?" Mrs. Conde asked Javier, ignoring

me completely. Then she turned to me. "How are things at home? It's just the three of you? Your mother works full-time, your father's not around?"

"We do okay. He's not abused at home, if that's what you're implying." I said that in response to the judgmental look.

"That wasn't what I was implying," Mrs. Conde snapped, revealing that she herself was a carrier of pent-up anger. She leaned back in her chair and crossed her arms. She kept her eyes on Javier, studying him. What made him the way he was? If she was waiting for an answer to that question, she was going to wrinkle up and wither before our eyes. "I just don't see any remorse for what you did to Alicia Flores." Javier kept his eyes down. At least he was no longer glaring at Mrs. Conde.

"He's already said he won't hit anyone. Can he go back to school now?"

Mrs. Conde ignored me. "I want you to attend the M and F—Mind and Fitness—class at the Carballo Rec Center. It's from three to five on weekdays and ten to twelve on Saturdays. It's four weeks long. It started yesterday but you can go today. Joseph Delgado, who runs the program, is a recently retired detective from the forty-first precinct. Kids in his class learn self-control through different activities like role-playing, team building, competitive exercise."

"No way." All things considered this was a very clean and mild response from Javier.

"What happens after he goes to class?" I asked.

"I'll consult with Joseph next week. Then I'll talk to Javier again. Hopefully we can come up with a plan that's good for Javier and everyone concerned."

"Can I speak with my brother for a second?"

Mrs. Conde looked at me as if to say *make it work* and then left the room and closed the door. I noticed for the first time that the door was half glass and half wood.

"The woman has issues," Javier said.

"I would too if I worked here." I looked around the bare walls and saw a white radiator, the source of the stifling heat. I stretched out my legs and exhaled loudly. "I don't know what to do here. I'm stuck."

"I don't need no school. I be awright."

"Yeah. Look, I need you to stay in school while Mami's going through all this. I'll pay you to go to school and to this Mind and Fitness class."

"What they do there?"

"Most likely the guy who teaches it is going to scare you into not breaking any rules and laws. You might get taken to a prison or something, so you know where you might end up."

Javier grinned. He saw I was trying to make the class hard to refuse. Before he could say no, I took out of my wallet the one-hundred-dollar bill that I had taken from Alma. "You can buy a new video game with this. Just show up and pretend you're interested. How hard can that be? There'll be more money like this. I'm working on something."

"With Primo?"

"Yeah."

Javier grabbed the bill and stashed it in his pocket. "I'm only doing this because Primo told me to go along with you. I'm X-Teca now. The X-Tecas are my family, not you."

"All right! I don't want you to be family either!" The words came out with a force I did not know was there.

Javier looked at me, stunned. Then he recovered and said: "And don't tell anyone I'm taking classes for my mind or whatever. Not even Alma. I don't want no one to know."

"You got it. No mind classes for you. So you'll show up there this afternoon. You know where the rec center is, right? Three o'clock. And you'll get yourself to school?" I tried to sound brotherly again but I don't think I succeeded.

"Yeah, man. Don't sweat it. Go on and booze it up."

160

Wednesday, February 22

I found her on an empty lot on Edgewater Road near Riverside Park. Mimi and two other women were huddled around a rusty barrel where they had built a fire. She came over when I called her name. I was surprised she recognized me.

"You the kid gave me the weed," she said when I lowered the window. "What you doing here?"

"I just have some questions. I'll pay you." Earlier that day I had cashed Julia's paycheck for her last two weeks of work. I opened my wallet and offered Mimi twenty dollars. She took the twenty I offered and grabbed another twenty from my wallet.

"Ten minutes." She went around and climbed in the truck and took off the same fake-fur jacket from the other day "What kind of questions?"

I drove a couple of blocks and then stopped behind an empty trailer. "I can't drive and talk at the same time."

"Okay, but keep the motor running." Mimi cracked her window and lit a cigarette. "Ask away."

"A friend of mine died last year. It was ruled an accidental overdose. Heroin. But . . . it all happened so fast. A month after she graduated. There were no signs she was using. How can there not be any signs? No one saw any marks." I glanced at Mimi's arms. She crossed them to keep them from my sight.

Mimi looked at me for a long time as if trying to figure out what I *really* wanted to know. She took a long drag of her cigarette and then exhaled in the direction of the window. "She may not've been shooting veins. To shoot a vein with H . . . it takes a while to get there. People start off snorting it. Or you can just pop a hit under the skin." Mimi pinched the skin on her hand and lifted it. "Or you can punch it in a muscle. You can overdose no matter how you get it in. You don't even have to be addicted to die from it."

"Wouldn't there be some signs?"

Mimi opened her window and flicked her cigarette out. "Shooting smack is most times something you work your way up to—you know, you keep wanting more of that good feeling and it gets harder and harder to get. But there no rules. Someone knew she was getting high, that's for sure. Who was your friend hanging with? It takes a village to make a junkie, they say."

"No one . . . she broke up with her boyfriend June sixteenth. Then she's found dead July twenty-third. The times I saw her before she died, I didn't notice anything. It wasn't just me that had no clue. No one suspected she was using."

"Most friends and family don't want to see what's right in front of their noses, know what I mean? Not all addicts fit the picture of a loser you have in your head. Your friend, even if she didn't show it, was probably more like me than you think."

I shook my head. Rosario was no junkie. There was no way that Rosario and Mimi shared the same universe. There was world of difference between them.

"You're judging me." Mimi said fiercely.

"No."

"The only difference between her and me is I'm just luckier." Mimi opened the door and then closed it again. "Let me tell you something. Everyone's addicted to something. Everyone's looking for a high one way or another. You hankering for your girl all this time is no different than me shooting up. She's your high and you're chasing it." She glowered at me for a few moments and then opened the door again and stepped out.

I watched her walk away until she turned onto Edgewater Road again. *Hankering*, the word she used to describe what I felt for Rosario, was one I hadn't heard in a long time. One of those words that sound like what they mean. Inside, around the area of my chest, I could feel and hear the hankering.

Thursday, February 23

Today at school, I went around making excuses for being absent and getting permission to do my schoolwork from home. I tried not to dramatize Julia's illness—all I had to do was mention "tumors" to receive compassion and pity. Afterward, I walked over to Mr. Cortazar's classroom. I stopped outside the door to collect myself. What I wanted to know most of all was what he and Rosario talked about during that last call. What was her state of mind? If Rosario had called me instead, I'd know if she was in a bad state.

"Whoever is outside lurking, come in and get it over with." It was Mr. Cortazar shouting from inside the classroom.

I stepped into the brightly lit room. Mr. Cortazar was

sitting at his old wooden desk, a stack of blue composition books in front of him. "I wasn't lurking," I said, embarrassed.

"Nico!" Mr. Cortazar stood, walked over to me, grabbed both shoulders, and gently shook me. "It's good to see you. How are you? How's your mother? Alma said she was in the hospital."

"It doesn't look good." Mr. Cortazar led me to one of the student desks and sat me down. He moved another desk and sat down in front of me. I could tell he was waiting for me to give him more information. "The tumors in her lungs are advanced." Somehow that sounded better than calling the tumors malignant.

"I'm so sorry."

There he was again, with that face that said, *Tell me all your secrets and all your sins, confidentiality and forgiveness are guaranteed.* I needed to change the mood of the conversation quickly before I emptied out my heart. "I've been making arrangements with my teachers to work from home."

"Sure, sure. You keeping up with your journal?"

I laughed. "Yes."

"What's so funny?"

"It's . . . I spend a lot of time on it . . . every day. Long entries. Most of them. A journal on steroids, I call it."

"Are you being honest in your writing?"

I thought immediately of his novel, which I had started to read. The story starts with a man on death row remembering the events that eventually got him where he was. I had to stop after the first ten pages. Each sentence was a puzzle I struggled to put together before an image appeared. I had the feeling the author was writing something only a few could appreciate. I wasn't one of them. There may have been honesty there, but I couldn't get to any beauty.

"Nico, are you all right?"

I waited a few more seconds and then I decided that this moment demanded some attempt at truth. "Remember that story Rosario wrote? It was called 'Fragmentation.' About the nurse in an old people's home who neglected her own parents. There was something truthful about it even though I know for a fact it was not autobiographical. Was that what you mean by honest writing?"

There was a startled look on Mr. Cortazar's face. He took his glasses off and squeezed the top of his nose with his thumb and index finger. Finally, he said, "Yes, when we read that story, we recognize a truth about the human condition. The nurse's hypocrisy, her shame at the duplicity of her life; all of Rosario's stories had that kind of emotional honesty in them—a connection between who she was, what mattered to her, and how she wrote. Did you read them—her stories?"

"She only let me read that one."

"Ah."

Mr. Cortazar waited for an explanation, and for a moment I was tempted to give him one. I didn't. He might've been a magnet for secrets, but he was not going to get mine. After a long silence, Mr. Cortazar asked, "Is there something on your mind?"

I took a deep breath, looked into his eyes. "Rosario. She called you . . . the night she died. You were the last person she called."

Mr. Cortazar sat suddenly upright, as if my question had sent a bolt of electricity up his spine. He looked into my eyes, and I forced myself not to blink. When he finally spoke, it was with the tone of someone who resents being asked a personal question by a stranger: "And you want to know why me?"

"I'm trying to understand why she died."

I could see him thinking, deciding whether I deserved to know the truth. When he spoke, it was with a teacher's voice, as if giving a lecture. "I had a special friendship with Rosario. I read her work, made editorial suggestions. In some cases, I acted as her literary agent, sending her book of stories to publishers I knew. I tried to be helpful to her . . . with her writing."

"A special friendship?" I asked. There was a jealous, accusing tone to my voice. The words just came out that way. I make no apologies.

Mr. Cortazar smiled as if to let me know that my reaction was perfectly understandable. "I was her mentor," he added. "That's what I meant by special."

"What did she sound like? You must have noticed her state of mind." I sounded peevish and petty. I seemed to have lost all ability to pretend.

Mr. Cortazar gripped the sides of the desk. I saw his Adam's apple travel up to the top of his neck and then slide down. He waited for me to meet his eyes and then said: "You don't know how often I replay that phone conversation in my mind. Did I miss something? Was she asking for help and I was too self-absorbed to catch the message behind the words? She called me to find out if I had heard from a place where I had sent her book."

"What did she say?"

Mr. Cortazar's lips trembled. His eyes reflected doubt and indecisiveness. The face of the composed teacher crumbled and now I saw a scared and lonely man. "She . . . just . . .

asked . . . for news. I had nothing new to report to her. I didn't detect anything. She sounded . . . disappointed . . . about not hearing anything . . . anxious. To hear good news. The usual disappointment at not knowing. That's all. Her reaction was . . . normal . . . expected. How we all respond to waiting about . . . whether our work is accepted."

There was something about the nervous way he spoke that made me think he was lying or hiding the truth. I stared at him. Waited for him. I was giving him a chance to redeem himself in my eyes. Students started to come into the room, but Mr. Cortazar remained frozen, his eyes on some invisible image behind me. I knew he was remembering Rosario. The look on his face was guilt. I recognized that look anywhere and on anyone. I started to lift myself out of the desk when he turned to me and said: "Nico. You want to know why she died. There's no answer to that."

I stared at him for a few seconds. I don't know why I felt so much anger at the man just then. I didn't want platitudes. And if there are no answers, there are at least beliefs. I wanted him to tell me the truth about Rosario, his truth as he saw it, about her last call to him. He was so big on honesty and yet he let a precious moment for honesty pass. I shook my head and walked out.

Friday, February 24

Conversation with Rosario.
Two months before Rosario's death.

SCHOOL LIBRARY

ME: (whispers) I don't understand why you won't let me read more of your stories. I loved the one you let me read. I'm the only friend you got that wants to write also, don't you think—

ROSARIO: (softly) Stop it, Nicolás. Don't ask me anymore. It will only make things worse.

ME: Make things worse? How?

ROSARIO: Nicolás! Don't ask silly questions. You know why.

ME: Please.

ROSARIO: I don't want us to have that kind of connection. Okay?

ME: What are you talking about?

ROSARIO: It will hurt . . . others. And you. And me.

ME: What are you afraid will happen? To you? To me?

ROSARIO: You know very well.

ME: It's too late.

ROSARIO: Then we need to make it unhappen.

Saturday, February 25

I was on my way to pick up Javier at the Carballo Rec Center when I recognized the name on the card I took from Alma's globe. Joseph Delgado was the same person who ran the Mind and Fitness class Javier was attending.

A woman at the entrance to the Carballo Center told me that Joseph Delgado was by the baseball field out back. I found him picking up small orange cones. I told him I was Javier's brother and asked him if Javier had showed up that afternoon.

"He was here. Left about half an hour ago." Joseph Delgado did not look like a retired police detective. He was a younger man than I had imagined. He had the crew cut and muscle-bulging build of a boxer. I waited a few moments for him to say more, but he seemed to have forgotten that I was standing there. He dropped the cones in a blue plastic barrel and then finally turned to me. "Got a second?" He pointed to a green wooden bench. When we were seated, he extended his hand to me. "Joseph Delgado." I gave him my hand and felt the crunch of his grip. I looked at his face and there was no malice there. The guy probably didn't know his own strength.

"Nico," I said, wiggling my fingers to see if the bones were still intact.

"Esther told me about Javier."

"Esther?"

"Esther Conde. The school counselor."

"Ah."

"I won't beat around the bush. Your brother's gonna end up either dead or in prison before he's fifteen. I don't even know if I'd give him that long."

"You think?" I didn't want to talk about the obvious. I wanted to ask about Rosario. Why did the police determine it was an accidental overdose?

"Yeah, okay, I'm only telling you what you already know, but you're gonna hear it again anyway. He was here all of ten minutes this morning before he got in a fight with a kid from Guatemala." I smiled. Now I understood why Javier was so eager to come to Mind and Fitness. "Yesterday we tried to play some flag football and he couldn't keep himself from tackling, not just the ball carrier but whoever got in front of him. I've seen violent kids before, but your brother is something else."

"Mrs. Conde told him to come here. You kicking him out?"

"No, I'm not kicking him out. I'm gonna work with him long as he shows up. But you gotta think long-term here. There's this school upstate, near Elmira. It's a middle grade and high school for at-risk kids, hard-core street kids like your brother, ex–gang members, many of them. Most are there because of a court order. They have a summer program. It'd be a good start. I can talk to your mother about it. There might be scholarships available."

"Can I ask you a question?"

"Go ahead."

"You were the detective who investigated the death of Rosario Zamora. Her death was ruled an accidental overdose . . ."

"Rosario Zamora. The name rings a bell. When she die?"

"Last July."

"Here in Hunts Point?"

"She died at a motel called the Stardust. In Queens."

"Oh, I remember. The 105th handles that part of Queens. But they asked for help because they were backed up and the girl was from here. My partner, Daniel Barrera, took that one. That was the month before I retired. I was riding desk, doing office work, on account of a bad back."

I showed him the card with his name on it. He looked at it and then turned it and read the back. "Where you get this?"

"From Rosario's sister."

"Dan must've gave her my card so they could get the personal effects found on the scene. That's something I was doing back then. Why you asking?"

"She was . . . my friend. Her death was ruled an accidental overdose. How is that determined? If there was no autopsy done?"

"There was no autopsy?" Joseph looked surprised.

"No. Is that unusual?"

Joseph shrugged. "It happens. The MLI can decide to skip it . . . if there's no evidence of foul play. Must be that in your friend's case, cause of death was clear cut."

"MLI?"

"Medical legal investigator—from the medical examiner's

office. They get called when drugs are involved. Most of the time a drug-related death gets autopsied, but . . . overdoses? So many of them. If there's no foul play and the drugs aren't tainted, autopsy can be skipped. You have a problem with how it was handled?"

Joseph must have been good at interrogating suspects because the way he asked was intimidating. What exactly was my problem with Rosario's death? "But how exactly does the MLI guy determine the overdose is accidental?"

Joseph nodded as if he finally understood the reason behind my questioning. "You mean, as opposed to intentional?"

"Yes."

When Joseph spoke again, his tone was different, as if he were sharing something personal with a longtime friend. "During the twenty-seven years I was on the force, I must have seen some two dozen overdose deaths. I mean, there's not much separating an overdose and suicide. In most cases, the addict has been suiciding for a long time. If there's no evidence of foul play and there's no note or other signs of the person's intent, the death is written as an accidental overdose. It's easier on the family."

"Maybe the heroin was tainted with something that killed her. An autopsy would have shown that, right?"

Joseph looked at me for a long time. "Yeah, an autopsy would have shown if it was bad dope. But any heroin found on the scene would have been sent to the forensics lab."

"And if it was tainted, the death would still be called accidental overdose?"

"Yeah, that part would stay the same. But we'd try to find out how it was obtained . . . to prevent further deaths. I don't remember any follow-up in this case. Probably the labs came back clean. How old was your friend?"

"Eighteen."

"Look, let's do this. I'll ask Dan about your friend. What the lab say about the dope and any details surrounding her death he remembers. I'll ask him and then call you. Meantime, you think about that school in Elmira for your brother. All right?"

"Okay." I stood with difficulty. My legs felt shaky.

Joseph stood as well. "Let me have your number." After I gave it to him, he said, "Javier's not lost . . . yet. We can still save him."

I walked slowly home as sunlight disappeared and the streetlights flicked on. What was it about my conversation with Joseph that hurt so much? *There's not much separating an overdose and suicide. In most cases, the addict has been sui-ciding for a long time.* Was that it? Rosario's life at some point turned into a suiciding no matter how you cut it?

When I got home, I read a text from Sabrina:

> Sabrina: At my mom's office. Come over?
>
> Me: Can't now. Maybe some other time?

A few seconds later came her response.

> Sabrina: Everything all right?
>
> Me: Yeah. Things.
>
> Sabrina: You want to send me your novel?
>
> Here's my email: sabrosa18@gmail.com

I put my phone on the kitchen table and stood there feeling . . . lost. What a word. Javier was not lost *yet*, according to Joseph Delgado. He meant we could keep him alive or out of jail. Javier might not be lost, but I sure as hell felt lost. I was lost as in I had no idea where to go next, as in it no longer mattered which way I went. One direction was as good or as bad as another. I ended up in my room somehow, not knowing how I got there. I hesitated one last moment and opened my laptop. I found the document I was looking for.

I typed: Here it is.

I forwarded Ruth's novel to Sabrina.

Sunday, February 26

Alma was in the process of putting a bag of frozen peas on Javier's eye when I got home from visiting Julia. It was around ten a.m. and she had come in to borrow some instant coffee when she found Javier. "This had nothing to do with the X-Tecas," she said before I could ask what happened.

Javier was sitting on the sofa. I removed the bag and inspected his nearly shut eye. The purple-and-black area around his eye was the size of a man's fist. "Can you see?"

Javier nodded and whacked my hand away at the same time. I moved closer and saw the swollen lip. The nose was red but not broken. "Can you talk?"

"No," he snapped, defiant.

"Do you know what happened?" I asked Alma.

"It's not totally his fault. He and Luis were playing video games at Zobo's and when they walked out, they ran into the uncle of the girl at school. The one he fought with couple of weeks ago."

"Why didn't you call me?" It occurred to me I had not even noticed that Javier had not shown up last night. "Where did you spend the night?"

"With Luis," Alma answered for him when Javier didn't respond.

"How old was this uncle who beat you up?" Javier closed his other eye and bit his lip. I wasn't going to get anything out of him. I turned to Alma.

"Thirtysomething?" she said reluctantly.

"What?" My blood boiled. I was angry, not so much at Javier as at everything. I moved about the room, looking for something to break.

Alma came next to me and forced me to sit down on a kitchen chair. "Don't make this any worser."

"Don't make this any worser," I mimicked, still fuming. I stood, grabbed a plastic cup from the sink, and filled it halfway with water. I found the bottle of aspirin in one of the

182

cabinets and shook out two pills. I went back to the sofa. "Take these," I told Javier. He grabbed the pills out of my hand and popped them into his mouth. He pulled himself out of the sofa. I grabbed his shoulders. "Why didn't you call me?" Javier didn't answer. I couldn't decipher what I saw in his face. It wasn't hatred, for once. It was more like he was embarrassed he got beat up by a thirtysomething man. It weighed on him to have the body of a twelve-year-old. He walked around me and limped to his room.

I sat on the sofa in front of Alma, calmer now. "Do you know where the uncle lives?"

"No, and you need to let Primo handle this. You got enough things to worry about right now."

"Primo?"

"The guy who hit Javier called Primo last night. Apologized. Says he got carried away. He saw Javier coming out of the recreation center and decided to confront him, tell him men don't hit girls, etcetera, but then Javier kicked him in the nuts and he lost it. That's what he's saying."

"How you know all this?"

"Ruben called me this morning. Primo told him about Javier."

"I don't like Primo fixing things for us."

183

"He's trying to help. Right now you need all the help you can get."

Her fixed stare said that my need for help involved more than just Javier. "I don't need help." I sounded bitter. "Why are you looking at me like that? What kind of help you think I need?"

She bit her lip. A sign she didn't want to say what she was thinking. Instead, she said: "What happened with Noah? He said you two had a face-to-face."

"We'll get over it."

"He told me it was about Rosario."

I sat up, started to walk toward the kitchen, then came back and sat on the edge of the sofa. "How do you know Rosario died of an overdose of heroin and not from bad junk? Did you ever get a tox report on the heroin?"

I was expecting Alma to be surprised at my question, or the timing of it, but she wasn't. "It was on the death certificate: accidental drug poisoning."

"What drug?"

"The police said it was heroin."

"But how did they know it wasn't something else, like fentanyl? Did they test it? Maybe it wasn't an overdose; maybe she injected something deadly by mistake?"

"Mami was the one talked to the police. They told her it was heroin. Too much of it at once is what they said. They called it accidental." Alma's cheeks reddened the way they do when she's about to cry. She was holding back tears when next she spoke. "You gotta let go of Rosario's death! My mom and me, Noah, we've all let go of the way she died. We haven't let go of Rosario, but we've let go of the way she died. Why not you?"

I took a deep breath. I had to stop talking, but I couldn't. I lacked control over the words spewing out. "Her death— what if none of it was her fault? Just a mistake, you know. Like you or I might make. I mean, sometimes I think I could make that kind of mistake."

I was pretty sure that Alma would not understand what I had said. Not a word of it. I myself couldn't understand the words that still floated in the air. But Alma did understand. I could tell by the look of kindness in her face. She stood quickly and said, "I'll be right back." She walked out of the apartment. I leaned back on the sofa and closed my eyes. It occurred to me that maybe the Rosario in my dream was also asking me to let her go. When I opened my eyes, Alma had taken one of the kitchen chairs and placed it in front of me.

She sat and handed me a small yellow sticky note. I took it from her hand and read.

> Hey babe, only the best snow white for you.
> Pay me later with your lovin the ways you do.
> See you in the twinkles.

I stared at the piece of paper forever, it seemed. Alma spoke: "I found it in a drawer of her desk. Whoever was giving her the dope wrote that." Alma waited for the words in the note to sink all the way, deep, as far as they could go. I forced myself to think, to push through the glob of pain in my chest and head and think. Of course, if Rosario was shooting up, she had to have a dealer, and since she didn't have money, she would have to find a way to pay for it. It was logical, but that didn't make it hurt less. I had never thought of Rosario like that—selling herself. My Rosario. I started to stand, but Alma held me down. She said softly, gently, comforting me as best she could, "I don't know what was so painful in Rosario's life she felt she had to escape it. She was a complicated person. She was. I know you don't want to hear this, but she was also at times selfish and cowardly. She didn't want to accept the crappy part of living."

I looked at Alma, expecting to find resentment or jealousy on her face. There was none. What she said about Rosario, she said out of love. For me or for Rosario, I couldn't tell which.

She went on, "You're complicated like her . . . in many ways. But you—you eventually face up to what needs to get done . . . even if it takes you a while to get there." She tugged at my ear.

"Ouch! Please go away," I said tenderly.

She stood up slowly, using my knee for leverage. "Call Noah."

"Why should I call *him*?" I said peevishly.

"You hurt him."

"Me? He accused me of trying to *be* like Rosario. Didn't even want me to *think* about her. Why is everyone so set to have her not only dead but forgotten?" I closed my eyes. No, I shut them. I didn't want to see Alma's reaction to what I had just said or the bitterness with which I said it.

I kept my eyes shut until I heard the door open and then close. I stretched out on the sofa and covered myself with the old afghan. I repeated Alma's words—*selfish and cowardly*—over and over again. The words were hard to accept or believe, but then, why should Rosario be any different than me?

When my head felt like it would explode, I jumped out

of the sofa and carefully folded Julia's afghan. I leaned my face against it. It smelled like Julia. I took a deep breath. The sticky note that Alma had brought was still on the table. I wondered if Alma had left it there on purpose as some kind of bitter medicine—to cure me of my "Rosario illness." I took the note and placed it in my wallet.

The thing about an illness is that sometimes it is better than nothing.

Monday, February 27

I don't know why I keep writing in this journal. There's no need to impress anyone anymore. Although if that's the case, why did I send Sabrina Ruth's novel pretending it was mine? There's something inside me that stinks of ME, ME, ME, and there's no way of getting rid of the stench.

Who am I writing this for? This journal's become like the notebook of those explorers stranded on the South Pole: *Seal blubber, enough for one more day. No hope left.*

What did I do today? I went to the fish market. Noah wasn't there. I don't know what I would have said to him if he was. I'm sure he knows how I feel about Rosario. Should I apologize for that?

Then after I finished cleaning up the fish bins, I talked to one of the drivers who I'd recruited to deal. He's ready to take some coke from me and sell it. But he didn't have the money to pay for it up front. He'll pay me after he sells the product. I called the second guy and it was the same with him. Coke and molly first, money follows. This, in ordinary circumstances, could have been one of those signals the universe sends you: Desist! Desist! Or maybe it was Rosario saying *follow me*. I chose what to hear.

It was still early when I drove over to the X-Tecas headquarters. The place was a stone structure with bars on all the lower windows and reinforced steel doors. Primo lived by himself on the top floor and his gang, some fifteen of them, occupied the rest of the property. One of the older X-Tecas, Rafito, was sitting on the front steps, smoking, and drinking from a Styrofoam cup.

"Here's Beef Wellington coming to visit the menudo folks," Rafito called out when I entered the small front yard. "If you're looking for your little bro, he ain't here."

"I'm looking for Primo." I tried to go around him, but he grabbed my ankle.

"Sit down for a sec, don't be rude. Primo's occupied with a

young lady right now. Take a load off." Rafito moved to make room next to him.

I sat down reluctantly. There was a white paper bag next to Rafito. He moved it to his other side when he saw me looking at the pistol inside it. "It's getting bad. Some putos from Cardona came by yesterday and shot at us." Rafito pointed to the lower front windows, which were now boarded up. "Why they go messin' with us? We didn't do nothin' to them. We respect their corners. Why they got to go looking for more? You know what I'm sayin'? It makes no sense." Rafito offered me a menthol cigarette. I took one out of the pack and lighted it with his lighter. I coughed a few times and Rafito laughed. "How long since you smoked?"

"About five years," I said.

"Here. Take a sip. It'll warm you up."

I grabbed the Styrofoam cup and drank. There was something sweet and soothing about the taste of rum and coffee. We sat in silence, taking turns drinking from the cup. Rafito watched the cars that entered the street. He stuck his hand into the paper bag whenever he saw a car he didn't recognize. "Can I ask you something?"

"Shoot," Rafito answered, his eyes on a red Lexus.

I was prepared to jump off the steps and hide behind an old

couch in front of the house if I saw any of the car's windows roll down. When the car had gone by, I asked my question. "You ever wish you didn't have to be worried all the time— somebody putting a bullet in you?"

Rafito gave me the kind of look you give someone who asks a question with a dangerous answer. "Pssh. It's what it is, man." Rafito spat. "What kind of question is that?" Just when I thought he wasn't going to say anything else, he spoke quietly. "It's tough bein' Mexican with all these other pende-jos trying to get in the action. There's vatos from countries I didn't know existed. Para-Gooay? Ecua-door? Who they? Why they pickin' Hunts Point? It's tough holding on. They ain't many of us. We gotta be strong and seem strong. Is all about not bein' weak. Con huevos, que no?" Rafito turned to look at the door behind him to make sure no one was coming out. "Listen, you know who got weak? Ruben. Alma and you tight, right?"

"Yeah."

"Vatos losin' respect for Ruben cause of her. If you gotta any pull with her . . . tell her she don't belong here. She's mak-ing things bad for Ruben. Everyone knows she don't like us. Thinks she's better than us. She's not like her sister, Rosario. Rosario be cool. She didn't have no judgment against us."

I don't know whether it was the cigarette and the rum, or Rafito mentioning Rosario, but I felt a wave of nausea come on. I flicked the cigarette away. I had to find a way to control the anger rising in me. "Rosario?" I tried to sound uninterested. "You knew her?"

Rafito nodded. "Oh yeah!" The grin on Rafito's face alluded to more he was willing to say. Then, maybe in response to the questioning look on my face: "Rosario was a looker. Alma too, I'll give her that."

The familiar way that Rafito spoke about Rosario made me angry. Rosario's name and memory did not belong in the minds and lips of people like Rafito.

"You okay, Beef Wellington? You turned white."

"I'm going in. The hell with it." I started to stand but Rafito grabbed my arm and pulled me back down.

"Relax, bro. He'll be done soon enough. Primo's cultivatin' a honey—you don't want to intrude on that." Rafito let go of my arm when he saw I wasn't moving.

"Cultivating?"

Rafito laughed and a small cloud of smoke came out of his mouth. "Yeah, man. Cultivatin'. See, Wellington, you not as smart as you think. Cultivatin' babes. That's Primo's signature, man. His brand. He's got the music they like. I don't know how he does it, but he hooks them to him, but hard, like they think it's real love, man. Smart ones too, don't think he doesn't. They his. By the time he drops them, they're hardcore or muling for us. He's got the touch with the bitches, man, know what I'm sayin'? Anyways, whatever you wanna say to him, you can say to me."

I looked at Rafito. He was in his midthirties, older than Primo and Ruben. If longevity was the rule, he would be in command of the X-Teca organization, but that rank was held by Primo, who inspired fear and respect in a way that Rafito never could. Would Javier grow to be a Rafito or a Primo? It was a crazy thing to take pride in, but I thought my little brother would be more like Primo. I snapped out of my reverie and said, "I got couple of guys willing to distribute in the city. Fancy restaurants. I need some product."

"Yeah?" Rafito asked. "You got it all set up?"

"I just need some stuff."

"You got cash? How much you want?"

"I'll pay for the product from the sales."

Rafito rubbed the top of his bald head with his hand. "You kiddin', right? Man, don't come to Primo with a deal's not cooked. You wastin' everyone's time. What's there to talk about?"

"I was hoping to get an advance."

"Advance? What? You think Primo's some ATM? I've known you since you were a kid getting beat up by your stepfather. 'Member?" I nodded. "You don't want to be owing Primo money. Okay? Damn! You lucky I talked to you before you saw Primo. I'm saying this for your own good and your little brother's. Come back with some cash, man."

"Yeah," I said. There was no way I could get past Rafito. "You're right. I'll go set it up and come back."

He dug into his pocket and took out a roll of bills. "Here, for your mamita. I heard she was in the hospital."

I looked at Rafito. It seemed wrong for him to mention my mother, for him to be concerned with her. The two worlds, my mother's world of honest work and Rafito's world, should not come in contact with each other. Yet there I was in the middle of both. Okay, maybe more and more in Rafito's world, and less and less in my mother's.

I took the five twenty-dollar bills that Rafito offered me. He would have been offended if I didn't take the money. The primary rule of social interaction with the X-Tecas: Know what can give offense and refrain from doing it. "Gracias. I'll be back with some money. Keep an eye on Javier when he comes around."

"Hey." Rafito motioned for me to come closer. "That brother of yours, Javier."

"Yeah?"

"He's got the biggest balls I've ever seen on a kid his age. Primo's taken him under his wing. He's cultivatin' him to be an enforcer. He's gonna be a good one too. The kid owns no fear."

I had this crazy image of Javier sticking his head out of the moist soil of a garden and Primo pouring water on him from a can. I smiled and said out loud, "Primo, the cultivator of women and kids."

"What you say?"

"Nothing. Just talking to myself."

"Why you think you're such a big mierda?" Rafito's mood turned instantly dark. "You too good for us, Beef Wellington?" Rafito dug out the black, sleek, expensive-looking pistol from the paper bag and pointed it at me.

Looking at that gun, which seemed like a beautiful piece of machinery, I had a strange sensation that I was looking at the instrument of my death. It was a déjà vu kind of feeling. Rafito was right. I did think of myself as better than him and all the rest of the X-Tecas. Yet there I was selling their dope.

"Correcto mundo, brother. I think I'm a big mierda," I said

contritely. I opened my arms and moved closer to the gun. "Go ahead and put me out of my misery."

I waited for Rafito to shoot. Instead, he said, "Get outta here."

After my mini encounter with death at X-Tecas' headquarters, I walked over to the Carballo Rec Center. The day, cold and gray, reflected how I felt. I had stood in front of a gun without an iota of fear. Was it because I was sure Rafito would not shoot?

Tell the truth, Nico. Part of you wanted him to pull the trigger.

Tuesday, February 28

D rove to Yonkers to get money from my so-called father. Money to buy cocaine from Primo and then sell it. If you asked why I was doing that, I don't know I'd have an answer. I was driving to Emir's to get money to buy drugs myself driven by a wacky energy that needed to be used not caring how or where.

I walked through the dimly lit showroom of Demirci's Emporium. It was one large, dusty room with rolls of carpet occupying almost every square inch of space. The only furniture was a huge wooden platform in the back where a carpet could be unrolled. On the ceiling above the table were soft-glow spotlights. A few feet to the right of that table was a door that led to Emir's office and his home away from home. I knocked three times, firmly, with resolve.

"What is it now?" Emir growled from inside.

"It's Nico!" I stopped myself from adding *your son* in case he had forgotten he had one.

"Door's open," I heard Emir say after a long pause. Emir's welcoming gesture consisted of swiveling on his chair to face me. He had grown a small goatee since the last time I saw him almost a year ago. "To what do I owe this pleasure?" But everything in his voice and face and body indicated that my visit was anything but a pleasure.

The feeling of disappointment I felt just then took me by surprise. I wasn't expecting a fatherly embrace by any means, but the coldness and distance of his voice unexpectedly whacked me. I silently berated myself for still feeling hurt. When did Emir walk out of our lives? Thirteen years ago. How much time had I spent with him since then? Maybe a couple of hours every year. And still there was a sore spot in me? "I need you to pay what you owe," I said angrily— because anger feels a hell of a lot better than rejection.

Emir pointed to the sofa on the side of the office. I shook my head. I didn't want to sit down. I forgot why I was there. Money. Money for what? Cocaine. I couldn't tell him that.

Julia. That's it. Julia. *Lie. Say it's about Julia.* "Mami's in the hospital. It's serious. I need money to take care of her. I need you to pay up what you owe us."

Emir made a shocked face. "I am sorry for Julia, but what is it you think I owe you?" His voice dripped with faked kindness.

"Past child support. You started paying child support when I was ten years old. Six years after you left." I felt my arms tremble. I had not expected losing all composure the way it was happening just then. I went to the sofa and sat on the edge before my legs gave out and I slumped to the floor.

Emir stood and walked to the small refrigerator on the other side of his desk. He bent down and took out a can of ginger ale. He took the lid off and handed the can to me. "Drink this. Take off your coat, it's hot in here."

I took the can from him and sipped the cold, bubbly liquid. I noticed for the first time that Emir was wearing a white short-sleeved shirt. It wasn't hot in his office—it was steaming. I could feel beads of sweat roll down my back. Emir went back to his chair and then rolled forward on it so that his knees were almost touching mine.

"So," Emir said, clasping his hands, "let's talk about this

like grown men.. You sure you don't want to take off your jacket? You look uncomfortable."

I *was* uncomfortable, but I did not take off my jacket. Taking off my jacket meant accepting a phony invitation at intimacy that I did not want to accept. "Just get on with it."

"All right, well. As to not paying child support early on, I respond this way. I was not sure you were my flesh and blood. Your mother, as you know, started an extramarital affair while we were married."

I gulped down the remaining ginger ale in the can. I was getting dizzy. Trying to keep up with Emir's argument and thinking of the ways to refute it was also making me nauseous. I started to recite facts like a robot. "Fernando was in jail when she was pregnant with me."

Emir pointed to a massive black safe in the corner of the room. "In there I have a letter from your mother to this Fernando addressed to him at Rikers."

I glowered at Emir with all the hatred in my being. I could not believe that the son of a bitch had shown up in the dream of my funeral. I had to tell Noah to keep him out at all costs. He had no right to be there, the cheap, lying bastard. I tried to stand. Coming to see Emir had been a big mistake. That he and I were flesh and blood, as Emir liked to say, was incomprehensible to me, a source of everlasting shame.

"Relax, relax," Emir said, pushing me gently down. "Let's chat for a second, man to man. I only bring up uncomfortable matters to explain my point of view. I was . . . dishonored."

I had to look away from him so that that my words could come out in an intelligible order. When I spoke, it was as if I were reading from an invisible teleprompter. "You had to pay for all the back child support you owed. A couple of hundred each month in addition to the regular monthly payment until all was paid. You never paid a single dime." Then I looked at Emir. He was grinning, like a child who has been caught doing something naughty but knows he won't be punished. "You want to talk man to man?" I continued. "This man is calling you a cheat and a coward." I said this without anger. I was exhausted and all I wanted to do was leave the stifling heat of the room and feel the cold on my face once again. With any luck, it would be raining and I could let the freezing wetness numb me.

Emir's grin faded and a serious scowl appeared on his face. "Your mother's unfaithfulness ended any obligation I had for support . . ."

I waited for Emir to smile or indicate somehow that he was

joking, that his reverent, sanctimonious tone was a charade. What exactly did I expect would happen at this meeting? I felt so foolish for the spark of hope I felt sometimes. Hope for what? Hope that Emir had a drop of fatherhood in him. I stood, squeezed past Emir's legs, and made my way to the door.

"Hold on, Nico. Let's discuss this like . . ."

I turned and shouted, "Go to hell! Just go to hell!"

Emir was making the universal *slow down* motion with his palms. He had an amused grin on his face as if he were witnessing the harmless tantrum of a four-year-old. He stood and took a wad of bills from his right pocket. He separated five or six bills and offered them to me. "Let me at least give you a little something."

I stormed out of the room and ran to the street. I don't believe in the angels and spirits that Julia believed in, but I had no other way of explaining the force that kept me from striking Emir at that moment. *Something* held my hands and my feet. Along with the power that kept me from striking Emir came the thought that I was lucky I grew up without Emir's selfishness and hardness, all things considered.

I drove not knowing where I was going until I saw Dock Street and took that until I ended up in a park. I got out of the truck and walked on a path adjoining the Hudson River. There was ice on the New York and New Jersey shores, but there was a large, deep channel in the middle where the river moved freely toward the ocean somewhere at the end of Manhattan. A tugboat was making its way upstate. The freezing wind coming from the river stung my face with a strange heat— almost like one of Fernando's slaps. I could not remember whether Emir had ever hit me. Julia never openly complained about Emir. Once I asked her if marrying him had been a mistake. That's when she said to me the words I clung to and will cling to for the rest of my short life: *How could it be a mistake if you were born?*

There, watching the sluggish brown water of the river, I remembered the time that I was in eighth grade when Rosario came to our apartment to bring us some mofongo that Mrs. Zamora had made. I was sitting next to Javier at our kitchen table, working with him on one of his homework assignments. As soon as Javier saw that my attention was taken by Rosario, he bolted from the table and went to his room.

"Subtraction," I said when Rosario looked over my shoulder. "It's no use. The kid hates school and anything to do with it."

Rosario placed the plastic container with the mofongo in

the refrigerator and then pulled out a chair and sat across from me. My heart lit up like it always did when I had Rosario to myself.

"You know what happens to kids when they grow up without a father, like Javier or like you, or like me?" It was just like Rosario to dive straight into a serious conversation.

I tried to think of something I could say that would keep Rosario sitting there, talking adult stuff with me. All I could do was ask, "What?"

"They grow up missing something, with an emptiness they try to fill in different ways—ways that are never enough or even that good."

"Your father . . ."

"He was around until Mom got pregnant with Alma. And he wasn't much of a father for the year he was with us. Alma's father no one's seen. And Pepito's?" Rosario's face darkened. "That guy was an animal."

After a few moments, I thought of something I could say. "How do you fill it, then—the emptiness?"

Rosario smiled that beautiful, sad smile she sometimes allowed me to see. The smile that let me know in no uncertain way she saw in me a likeness of her soul. "Oh, I don't know . . . nothing that's working." She stood up quickly, as if realizing she had shared too much. "Got to go, Nicolás. Don't ever be a bad father or a bad brother, okay?"

This is what I discovered today: that I, Emir's son was, like my father. I remembered that, in my anger, I had called Emir a cheat and a coward. The truth the river tossed up at me just then was to see clearly that the apple did not fall far from the tree. I was a cheat and a coward like Emir. What else would you call the person who sent Ruth's novel to Sabrina? Or the person who wanted to run far away from Julia and Javier?

Cheat. Coward. The canicas that rattled inside me.

Wednesday, March 1

The Stardust Hotel in Queens. Two floors. Fifteen rooms on each floor. Forty-five dollars a day. A sign tall enough to be seen by drivers on the Van Wyck Expressway flashed the name of the motel in white neon letters. Beneath that in red: FREE X VIDEOS. I parked in front of room 3. In which of those thirty cheap rooms did Rosario live out her last moments? Looking at those yellow cinder-block walls and green doors, at the dirty flowery curtains behind the greasy windows, I thought this was where you came when every drop of beauty had been drained out of your world.

Why was I there? What did I expect to find? A door opened and a woman wearing only an oversize New York Mets T-shirt walked out with an ice bucket on one hand and a lit cigarette on the other. The cold made the woman hug herself. A man shouted from inside the room and the woman turned around and slammed the door shut. When she returned from the ice machine our eyes met. Only then did I notice that she was old and frail. She winked at me as she closed the door.

What was I doing there? I could rent a room. I still had the one hundred dollars that Rafito had given me. Maybe I could see and feel what Rosario saw and felt. But was that necessary? Just looking at the outside seediness of the Stardust was enough for me to know that Rosario had to be low on herself to end up there. I took out the sticky note that Alma had given me and read it again.

Hey babe, only the best snow white for you.
Pay me later with your lovin the ways you do.
See you in the twinkles.

Was "the twinkles" a reference to the Stardust Hotel? The image of Rosario paying for heroin with her "lovin" was so unbearable that I had to get out of the truck and breathe the cold air. The freezing wind soothed the dark imaginings taking place in my head.

"Hey, you can't park there if you don't pay for a room!" An old, skinny man wrapped in a yellow wool blanket had come out of the office and was motioning me to go away.

I walked up to him as I took out my wallet and we walked into the office. The Stardust's reception area was a small, cluttered room with a counter. A doorway behind the counter led to a bedroom where a TV was on. I could also see an unmade bed and a microwave back there. "You live here?" I asked, with possibly a tone of disgust in my voice.

"What's it to you?" the man said, going behind the counter. "Sixty bucks."

"The sign says forty-five," I replied.

"It's an old amount. I haven't had a chance to change it." He slid me a key attached to a plastic key holder with the number 22 written on it.

"I have some questions about someone who died in one of your rooms." I handed him three twenty-dollar bills.

He took the money and sneered, "More people bit the dust in those rooms I can remember."

"Last July. A young woman. Police said it was an accidental overdose."

I could see by the concentration in his eyes he remembered. "What about it?"

"Did you find her?"

"Luisa finds them. She does the rooms. I go look. To make sure they're dead. Then I call the cops."

I was still holding my wallet in my hands. I took out another twenty-dollar bill and slid it across the counter. "What you see?"

"What you lookin' for?" He took the twenty-dollar bill and slipped into his pocket.

I hesitated. "I want to know whether . . . the police ruled out foul play. They called it an accidental overdose."

The old man's forehead wrinkled and then he grinned. "There wasn't no foul play, I'll tell you that." The old man pointed at a TV monitor hanging from the ceiling. "CCTV. Police checked. No one came in or out after the guy she was with left around eight. She was alive when he left. Film shows her closing the door after him. Luisa found her around noon next day."

"Someone was with her around eight?"

"Sure. The police took the film showing a guy coming in around six and leaving at eight."

"Who?" My heart was pounding. "Did you see the film? Had you seen the guy before?"

"I can't tell one john for another. They all look the same."

"She wasn't a prostitute," I said defensively.

"If you say so." Then, a smile. "I tell you why I remembered this one. When I went into the room, I saw her on the bed, the needle and junkie stuff next to her, but there was a noise coming from the bathroom. I walk in there and there's a laptop in the sink with water running over it. It wasn't like it was on the edge and it slipped or anything. It was dumped in there with the screen open so water zapped the hard drive."

"Her laptop."

"You want? I can let you have room twelve. That's where . . . it's vacant."

"No." I gave him back the key to room 22.

I walked out and sat in the truck. I let the cold numb me. Rosario ran water over her laptop. Her writing. Her dreams. That's when her hope ended. Whatever happened afterward was incidental.

Thursday, March 2

Julia was sitting up in bed listening to Harrison read from the legal documents he had prepared. Harrison stopped when he saw Julia stretch her arms toward me. I approached slowly, shocked at the changes that were taking place in her body. The skin over her cheekbones had shrunk and her eyes had sunk deeper into her head so that it was now possible to see the outlines of a skull. This was my mother, my beautiful mother, transforming into one of those skeleton masks people wear on Día de los Muertos.

Standing there, looking at the face that was once so striking, it hit me for the first time that Julia was going to die. I don't know what I thought of before, but her death did not become real until that moment. It's as if the knowledge of her impending death had to descend from my head to my gut for me to accept it.

When we finished hugging, Julia said, her voice a raspy whisper: "Harrison took care of all the paperwork. Mrs. Zamora will be your guardian and Javier's until your birthday next month, and then you'll be Javier's guardian."

"You'll be around next month." I said this with a cheerfulness that was obviously fake.

Julia turned to Harrison. "Can we sign these this morning?"

Harrison stood quickly, avoiding my eyes. "I'll go find two witnesses and a notary."

"You're a notary," Julia said.

"With these kinds of documents, it's best to have all the officials be unrelated." Harrison stacked all the papers neatly on the table and walked out of the room, still without once looking at me.

"What's up with him?" I asked Julia when he was out of the room.

"Can you push my bed down? There's a button some-place." I lowered the back part of the bed and then fluffed her two pillows. "I need to go home, Nico. I don't want to die here."

"I'll work on it. We have to line up home care with people who can give you the medicine you need."

"And clean my bum," Julia said sadly. "I didn't think it was going to be so soon." I dipped my index finger in a glass half-full of water and touched Julia's chapped lips. When I finished, she stuck out her tongue. "What color is it?"

"Like you been eating chalk."

"Yuck. Go see Fernando. He'll help us out. He's a good man deep down." That was Julia's refrain about Fernando. The man regularly beat her and Javier and me and was unfaithful to her almost from the start of their relationship, but if you told her something nice about Fernando, she'd believe it. "Maybe he'll come see me?"

I could only stare at Julia silently. There were lies and then there were lies. Giving her unrealistic hope seemed cruel. Julia made a wistful expression with her eyes and mouth as if to say that one can still dream of the impossible. "Ay!" Julia placed her hands on the sides of her abdomen.

"I'll get a nurse."

"They'll give me a shot and I want to be awake to sign the papers." She took my hand and pulled me down toward her.

"Nico . . . I never worried about you. All my worry has been for Javier . . . but that doesn't mean . . ."

"I know, I know. You don't have to say anything."

"I do have to say it. Let me say it. I'm so grateful for you. You're the best thing that happened in my life even if I don't hardly tell you."

"Mami, save your strength."

"I'm sorry. This is not fair to you." Julia clutched her head with both hands and grimaced. "Better go find Harrison."

I stayed long enough for Julia to sign the documents and then I left. Harrison caught up with me as I was about to step into the elevator. He handed me a manila envelope. "Consent to guardianship form to be signed by Javier's father. He needs to relinquish his rights as the most logical legal guardian."

I chuckled. "I don't think he'll object."

"Just to be on the safe side. The lawyer in my office who I drafted the guardianship docs thought it be a good idea."

I took the envelope from him and tucked it under my arm. "Thank you for doing all this."

"We'll keep the original will in my office. I'll send you copies by mail. I'll get the papers to a judge we work with. He's doing us a solid by pushing them to the top of the pile."

"All right." I was wondering why he couldn't give me the copies next time he saw me when he said quickly, sheepishly, "I wish I could do more. I just can't. I'm sorry." He pivoted quickly and walked back in the direction of Julia's room.

"Hey!" I shouted after him, waited for him to turn around. "What if something happens to me? We need to provide for a guardian to Javier if something happens to me."

There was a confused look on Harrison's face. "After you're Javier's guardian, you can sign another document. I'll send it to you."

"Thanks. The sooner the better. You never know."

Harrison studied me for a few moments. "Is there something . . ."

"No, man, no. Just covering all bases."

I left Harrison standing in the middle of the hospital corridor looking mystified. I hurried out of the hospital, wondering who Javier's guardian could be after I was gone. Mrs. Zamora? Could I do that to her and Alma? But who was I kidding, the true guardian of Javier when I wasn't around would be Primo, and Javier's family would be the X-Tecas. So why worry about a form?

Some days seem like they will never end, and some days go

by in a flash. The time texture of this day was slow, sluggish. There were all these things that I needed to do so that Julia could come home: talk to Dr. Zimmerman, go see Fernando, but I couldn't get myself to do any of them. Harrison's words began to beat inside me in a steady rhythm: *I just can't. I just can't. I just can't.* I had this overwhelming wish to forget everything for a few moments.

I had a manila envelope in my hand and I had no idea what it was. It took a few moments for the words *consent to guardianship form* to enter my mind. It took me another few moments to realize that the envelope was getting soaked by a cold, hard-pelting rain. People were running past me, seeking the protection of the hospital's entrance. I stuffed the envelope inside my jacket and walked toward the truck.

When I got to the truck, I took off my jacket and wiped the water from my head with a rag that I found under the seat. My teeth were chattering, and my shoulders were shaking. I turned the motor on. The cabin of the truck was a refuge, a capsule that protected me. I patted the dashboard like I would a faithful dog. After a long time, after the rain stopped and people began to hurry again on the sidewalks, I heard the ping of my cell phone and read Sabrina's text:

Wow! Just Wow! Your novel! I'm speechless!

Be good to see you.

Day after tomorrow? My mom's office. Around

noon.

I replied with a single word.

Yes.

Friday, March 3

Fernando and Sunny lived with their two kids in a ten-story apartment building. If I were ranking the place, I would give it two stars, whereas our apartment building wouldn't make it into any constellation. Fernando's building had a lobby with white mosaics that had been recently swept and mopped, and an elevator that worked. I figured the rent for their two-bedroom was in the two thousand range. In other words, there was enough money for child support if the will and decency had been there.

I took the elevator to the eighth floor and walked over to their apartment. There was a snowman holding a candy cane still glued to the door. I took a deep breath and reminded myself that both Fernando and Sunny were bullies who were aware of their power to intimidate and make weaker humans cower. I readied myself for the barrage of verbal (and possibly physical) violence that they would throw at me. I told myself I wasn't there to beg. I was there because Julia asked me to come and I wanted to be able to say to her that I'd tried. Also, ever since my visit to the Stardust I had this angry energy that wouldn't let me stand still. A visit to Sunny and Fernando's seemed like a good place to discharge the extra voltage.

"What do you want?" Those were the welcoming words of the lovely Sunny when she opened the door.

"I'm here to talk to Fernando."

"He's got nothing to say to you." She was about to slam the door on my face, but I pushed myself in. "I'm calling the cops."

"Go ahead." Sunny was a small, curvy woman. The top of her curly hair came up to my chest. I looked past her into the living room and the rooms in the back. "We can all talk to them about child support and about how you whipped Javier's back with a belt last time he was here."

Her lips twitched as if to lash out at me, but she controlled herself enough to sound semi-civil. "Fernando's not here anyways. So whatever you got to say, say it. I'll tell him." Sunny was wearing a full-bodied, flesh-colored spandex exercise suit that was way too revealing for a mother of two. How she got into it, I had no idea. I tried not to look at her, or at least, to keep my eyes above her neck. Sunny was one of those women you can't help looking in their direction. In terms of beauty, she did not hold a candle to the fine, delicate features of Julia. It was just like Fernando Rojas to prefer the loud and raunchy over the classy and elegant.

"Where the kids?" I asked. A TV filled almost an entire wall of the living room. On the screen, a group of women were doing yoga. I picked a brown velvet reclining chair and sat down. Sunny came around and stood next to me. I kept my eyes straight ahead on the TV.

"Not that it's any of your business, but Ramon's in preschool and Tato's in day care. If you're looking for money, there isn't any. All of my salary as an esthetician goes to paying for the kids' schools. What Fernando makes is for the rest." She took a step and stood in front of me. I noticed a small tear on the knee of her exercise suit and kept my eyes there.

"Esthetician," I repeated to myself. I didn't mean to sound insulting and the smile that followed wasn't consciously meant to be sarcastic. It was just a word that I always found humorous for some reason.

My smile, however, set off a fuse in Sunny. "Damn right,

esthetician! I went to beauty college for a whole year! It beats folding laundry. Any mula can do that! Now get the hell out of my house before I get Fernando's gun and shoot your ass!"

I craned my head to look around Sunny's legs. The yoga women were standing on one foot with their palms touching above their heads. I waited for the urge to strangle Sunny to dissipate. I thought of Julia rising through the ranks of Lux Linen to become a supervisor and, at $39,000 a year, the highest-paid employee in her group. When the rage flowing through my body somewhat dissipated, I said, "It's good to know Fernando has a gun. Is it registered? We can add that to the list of what we tell the police when they come." I don't know that much about the law, but I knew it's almost impossible for an ex-felon like Fernando to get a gun permit in New York.

Sunny made a grimace like she knew she had just said something she shouldn't have. She grabbed the remote from the coffee table and turned the TV off. "Why are you here? Tell me once and for all and then get out." She had her hands on her hips and was making an *I'm waiting* face.

I stood and moved far enough so that my hands were not within grappling range of her neck. I spoke calmly but with authority. "I don't trust you will deliver this message to

Fernando so if I don't hear from him by tomorrow, I'm going to go see him at work." I waited for Sunny to see how serious I was. When I saw the slight nod that she understood, I continued. "Julia, my mother, is very ill. If something happens to her, Javier will be Fernando's responsibility."

"That ain't happening!"

"I'm not here to debate with you. I'm telling you how things are. This has all been discussed with lawyers and social services. Javier has Fernando's last name. It's on his birth certificate like Fernando insisted. When Julia dies, he goes to the father."

"Eso no puede ser." Sunny sounded confused, frightened. "Fernando says Javier may not even be his. Your mother put the horns on Fernando just like she put them on your father."

I peered into Sunny's face. There were beads of sweat popping out from somewhere underneath the mass of black curls and streaking down her forehead. "Tell Fernando that there's only one way out of Javier coming to live with you."

I could tell that it pained Sunny to ask what it was, but she did. "What?"

"If someone else becomes Javier's guardian. Like me, for example. Julia would have to appoint the guardian while she's still alive. Thing is—the only way she'll do that is if Fernando

223

pays all back child support. Tell him that. He comes up with owed child support in, say, the coming week and Julia will appoint me or someone else as guardian. That's the choice you got—child support or Javier. Tell Fernando to call me. I want to make sure you gave him the message." I went around her and started to walk toward the door.

"That's crazy!" Sunny was walking behind me, shouting. "We ain't got that kind of money. It's thousands. That's not fair! Listen to me! I'm talking to you, you piece of . . ."

I turned quickly and pointed my index finger at the space between her eyes. "No! You're not calling me names!" I said sternly. "Tell Fernando to call me."

"He'll kill you and that little bastard before he gives you . . ."

Sunny was still yelling when I stepped out and slammed the door behind me. I leaned against a wall and listened to Sunny shout at Fernando over her cell phone. I had no doubt that Fernando would call me soon. He wouldn't want Sunny harassing him when he got home. I took the stairs instead of the elevator. I needed to move. It was probably best that Fernando wasn't there. If he had been there and talked about Julia the way Sunny did, I wouldn't have been able to control myself. I was taller than Fernando, but he was comfortable with violence. Javier was like his father in that respect.

I was just about to start the truck when Fernando called. I let my cell phone ring a few times before I answered.

"That was quick," I said by way of hello.

"What the hell, man? You wanna die young?" Fernando's words were cold and menacing, a relief compared to Sunny's scalding anger.

I summoned all the courage I could muster. "What's it going to be? Javier or child support?"

"I don't even know if that brat is mine. Your bitch mother was out fooling with someone like she was fooling with me when she was with your father." I gripped the steering wheel with one hand and placed the phone face down on the seat next to me. I counted to five. "You there? You still there?" Fernando's voice sounded far away.

I placed the phone next to my ear and tried to imitate someone mature and calm. "You gave Javier your last name. You're named as the father on his birth certificate." I was surprised I could sound so businesslike. This was what this was. Business. I reminded myself I was smarter than Fernando.

"That don't mean nothing. Listen to me, you come to my house again and I'm gonna extinct you, hear me?"

"Extinct me? I love it when you try to sound smart. You think I care what you do to me? Julia's dying. She's dying, you miserable excuse for a human! You irresponsible worm! You think I'm afraid of you?"

"You better be," Fernando said, but there was fear in his voice.

I took three deep breaths and then went on, still thinking about what I had just said. Julia was dying? Did it take facing up to Fernando to realize that? There it was, the certainty of Julia dying, real as my anger. "You don't think I can make life hard for you and for your wife and your little kids? You don't think I have people that can help me? Ever hear of my homies the X-Tecas?"

"You threatening me? Don't even . . ."

"I gotta go. Listen, you should be paying around $500 a month for child support. You've never paid a cent and Javier is twelve years old. Multiply twelve years by twelve, which is the number of months in a year, and then multiply that by five hundred. That's how much you owe for child support under the law."

"I didn't make no eighty thousand all those years! I only just got promoted here and before that, lots of years, I had no job, or worked for hardly nothing."

"Okay. I hear you. I'll tell you what. Let's make it an even twenty thousand. Twenty thousand and I'll be Javier's guardian. I won't go to social services. You won't hear from us again."

Fernando laughed. "What? You outta your mind?"

"I gotta go, man. Think about it. Talk it over with your Sunny bunny. Twenty thousand. Give me a call."

I turned the phone off because I knew he was going to keep on calling. I waited until my heart had slowed down a bit and then I drove. *Ever heard of my homies the X-Tecas?* Did I really say that? What a hypocrite I was. Hey, all was fair in love and child support.

Saturday, March 4, 3:15 a.m.

L etter to Rosario.

You won't believe what I did. I gave this girl a novel I didn't write and said it was mine. I don't know why. Lots of stuff I'm doing these days I don't know why. The person who wrote the novel, she used a pseudonym. I don't understand how anyone can write something so beautiful and not be interested in receiving her due of recognition. You and me? We wouldn't be capable of that kind of anonymity. We always wanted to be somebody. You wanted to stand out in the eyes of others. I wanted you to see me as someone special.

I wanted you to love me.

Where was I? So, yeah, the things happening in my life right now—well, I'm at the Stardust. Not the real one, the mental one. Not yet drowning my laptop, but almost there. I don't see the point of it all. I'm going through the motions—acting as if I care. One of the chairs in the dream is about to be emptied. Julia's. Remember how she used to make you laugh? And you her. You reminded her of something—a dream she had to let go. You lit a spark in her when she saw you. She was your buddy, wasn't she? Remember the time when you were fifteen and you came in crying and you and Julia went into her bedroom so you could talk in private.

When she found out you died, it was as if part of her died. For a while there, for weeks after you were gone, I could see her struggling to find a reason to keep going. I thought it was the sadness of losing you that filled her. But now I see she was also trying to figure out how she could go on with her poor life when you, with all your promise, couldn't.

Saturday, March 4, 10:10 p.m.

I drove to Fordham with a glob of guilt inside me. I felt like I was letting someone down, but who? And in any event, too bad, I was doing what I was doing. By the time I got to Fordham, the skies had turned dark and the lightning flashes in the distance reflected what was happening inside me. Then the snow came. I parked the truck and walked to Sabrina's mother's office like a robot whose movements were controlled by someone else.

The door to the office opened slightly when I knocked.

"Come in!" It was the voice of a woman, not Sabrina. Did I get the date, the time wrong? I was about to turn around and run out of there when the door fully opened. The woman in front of me was an older version of Sabrina. She had Sabrina's features, the ample forehead—the almond-shaped eyes, the high cheekbones—Sabrina's beauty toned down by age. She had a stern expression on her face that made me think she had found incriminating evidence of my last visit to her office.

"I'm . . . I was looking for Sabrina."

"You must be the famous Nico." She opened the door fully and gestured for me to come inside. "I'm Rebecca Mendoza, Sabrina's mother. Sit over there, Nico." She pointed at the sofa. "Sabrina went to the copy room. She'll be right back. Let's chat."

I should have been nervous, but after Sunny, this elegant woman in a shiny green dress didn't seem all that intimidating. Who cared if she didn't think I was good enough for her daughter; I had come prepared to never see Sabrina again. I could feel her evaluating gaze on me while I waited for her to speak.

"You live in Hunts Point?" There was an undertone of fear in the way she pronounced Hunts Point.

"Yes, ma'am," I said with unhidden pride. The hell with these rich people and their assumptions about a place and what it must be like to live there.

"And you want to be a writer?" It took me a few seconds to

see the connection between the two questions she had asked. How strange and how improbable that someone from Hunts Point would want to be a writer.

"I write . . . a little," I said. I wasn't sure I could say I *wanted* to be a writer anymore.

"I hear you're going to Sarah Lawrence in the fall?"

"I haven't heard from them yet."

"Mmm. Well, I'm sure you'll have no problems getting in with your talent."

"My talent?" What talent? My talent in lying and deception? Was the woman being sarcastic?

"I hope you don't mind, but Sabrina was so impressed with your novel, and with you, that she asked me to read a couple of chapters, which I did. Your writing is exceptional, it is. I didn't have time to read the whole novel, but I didn't have to. I have devoted my life to separating literary wheat from chaff, so to speak, and I know good writing when I see it."

Now for the first time I began to resent the woman's intrusiveness. I didn't want to lie anymore. I came to see Sabrina to reveal myself as a liar and to regain the kind of honesty I had this morning when I wrote the letter to Rosario.

"Thank you. I agree. It is good writing, but—"

"Wonderful! I like people with the courage of confidence."

She checked her wristwatch. "I have a class in five minutes so I'm going to make this quick. The novel is not only good writing, but perhaps even more important, I think you have a huge commercial success in your hands. I called a friend of mine, a senior editor at one of the major publishing houses, and she's dying to see it. I'm going to give you her name and email so you can send her the novel. Send it to her today. She's waiting for it." Sabrina's mother stood and went to her desk, where she tore a piece of paper from a notebook and began to write. "You'll need to lose the pseudonym, of course." She looked at me and grinned. "Nico Kardos is sexy. It'll sell."

This was the time for me to speak up. I'd like to think that the reason I sat there silent as a toad was because I didn't want to embarrass Sabrina in front of her mother. I'd like to think that it was not cowardice but logistics that allowed that elegant woman to see in me what wasn't there. The judgment with which she initially greeted me had vanished, and instead there was this warm acceptance that welcomed me into the folds of those select few men who were good enough for her daughter. And it felt good. So good, just then. To be accepted. I was somebody.

Sabrina stepped into the room with a stack of folders just

as her mother was handing me the piece of paper with the editor's name and address. "You two talk?"

"Briefly, but sufficiently," her mother said to Sabrina with a wink. "Make sure he sends the novel to Laura this afternoon." And then to me: "Sabrina will fill you in on the details. We're expecting you for dinner on Sunday. Not tomorrow—the following Sunday. My husband wants to meet you." Sabrina's mother grabbed a leather suitcase next to the desk, kissed Sabrina, and then looked at me, and said, like a teacher to a student: "Don't let me down."

"I'm so glad you got to meet my mother. And she obviously likes you." Sabrina hugged me and then led me by the hand to the famous sofa. Everything began to happen so fast. It was like a dream that jumps helter-skelter from one scene to another. Sabrina sat next to me, her two hands wrapped around mine. "You know, when I told my mother where you lived, she was very dubious about you. That's partly why I asked her to read the first chapter of your novel, to make sure she saw how special you are. But she still wanted to meet you before she approved. And she did. She wouldn't have mentioned dinner at our house on Sunday if she had any reservations about you."

"I don't see how she could've approved. I didn't get a chance to say anything . . ."

Sabrina laughed. "Yup, that's Mom." Then she saw the piece of paper in my other hand. "You should call Laura Benson right now. She's amazing. The authors she's published! Wow! And you're next. Nico Kardos. Where did you get that yucky name Briel Alexander?" Sabrina breathed on my neck and in my ear. Tingling shivers vibrated through my body. "On second thought," she whispered, "maybe you should wait an hour or so before you call her." Her lips touched mine.

Just then the memory of Rosario came to me. This time I remembered something Rosario said the last time I saw her, a few days before her death. I had totally forgotten her words until that moment when Sabrina kissed me.

I don't like it here, Nicolás. I never will. I'm trying, but I can't.

We were in her room lying side by side in her bed and I thought she was talking about Hunts Point, but there with Sabrina it came to me that by "here," Rosario meant life on this earth.

I pushed Sabrina gently away.

"Oh no. Oh no." Sabrina covered her mouth with her hands. "Did I just make a fool of myself?"

"No, no, you didn't. I'm flattered. But . . . there's . . . things happening to me . . ." I touched my right temple. "I'm not sure . . . it's not you."

"Do you want to make love? Would that help?"

It was a tender, giving offer. Wasn't the real reason I had come to lose myself in the radiance of her body? For she *was* radiant. I pulled her toward me and kissed her forehead softly. Then I left.

It came to me as I walked away that I didn't like it *here* either.

Sunday, March 5

J ulia came home this afternoon. Dr. Zimmerman released her to palliative care after I told him that my father had agreed to pay for any hospice costs not covered by Julia's health insurance. Who knew lying could be so easy? As soon as I got the okay from Dr. Zimmerman, I called a medical supplies store and rented a hospital bed. It was a cheap bed, the kind you crank by hand. The mattress was a green, water-resistant foam worn out from supporting dozens of sick and dying people.

Just before the ambulance arrived with Julia, Noah knocked on the door. "Alma said your mom's coming home. You need help setting up?" His tone was friendly but reserved.

"We good?" I asked, tentative.

Noah glared at me. "We need to talk."

"Yes," I said contritely. "But give me a little time."

"Okay," he said. "Don't wait too long. Is that your bed in the lobby?"

We lugged the bed up the stairs in an awkward silence. It was as if Rosario was there between us. I guess she had always been there, but now both of us recognized and admitted her presence. But there were things to do and gradually the silences between Noah and me grew less and less.

Mrs. Santini came with a vase of pink miniature roses and a bag of groceries. Alma decided to bake chocolate chip cookies in our oven so the apartment would smell like humans lived there and not like a couple of males, i.e., barely human. Noah helped me run a cable extension to Julia's room and we placed the television on top of a dresser.

When Julia arrived, there were people to greet her, and the apartment was clean and welcoming. Javier came out of his room and greeted Julia with what looked like a hug, which made Julia happy. When Julia was settled in her bed, we were all silent in that small, dark bedroom with a tiny window overlooking the street below. We didn't have to say anything. Each one of us understood why Julia insisted on being there for the last days of her life. That room in that ordinary building on that muddy street was home, the only place on earth where Julia had felt safe and loved.

The nurse from the hospice organization that Dr. Zimmerman called arrived fifteen minutes later. Roberta Callas was in her seventies, tall and bony, with a white scarf covering her bald head. She looked like death's personal assistant. She went into Julia's room to set up an intravenous drip and then immediately came out and asked if we had a bedpan. Noah and I stood there, silently accusing the other of forgetting to buy a bedpan.

"I'll go get the bedpan," Mrs. Santini said, ending the impasse between Noah and me. Then to Roberta: "Why don't you make me a list of other things we might need."

Alma, Noah, and I sat in the living room while Mrs. Santini and Noah went to get some things and Roberta administered to Julia behind closed doors.

"Smells good," I said.

"It's hard to hide the smell of dirty socks," Alma said. "Have you done any laundry since your mother went to the hospital?"

"Mmm. What? Laundry? Ahh . . ."

"Javier smelled a little ripe this morning," Noah added.

"Please, give me a break with the parental advice," I pleaded.

Alma jumped out of her chair and headed to the kitchen. She opened the door to the oven and took out the tray of cookies. The warmth from the open oven reached us and Noah and I both sank in our seats. She was opening and closing drawers when she asked: "Do you have something to lift the cookies from the tray?"

"Use a knife," I said absentmindedly. I went over to the radiator and stayed there touching it. My phone vibrated in my pocket. A text from Fernando. He was parked in front of our building with a check. He wanted me to bring the consent form and to hurry up because he was double-parked. I rushed to Julia's room and knocked. Roberta opened the door a small crack.

"Is she asleep?" I asked.

"She's dozing. I just finished aspirating her lungs. She needs rest. Where's the oxygen I told you to get?"

"It's on the way. Listen, I need her awake for ten more minutes. Ten minutes."

There must have been something in my tone that conveyed urgency or maybe even desperation because Roberta acquiesced with a small nod of her spectral head.

Noah and Alma were standing in the hall. "What is it?" they both asked.

"Javier's father is downstairs with a check. I'm going to try to get him to come up and see Julia."

"You got him to pay back child support?" Alma asked, impressed.

"I'm pretty sure it'll be a lot less than what he owes or what I told him." I ran to my room and grabbed the consent to guardianship form from my desk.

"Are you sure it's a good idea to bring that guy up here?" I could tell by her tone that Alma didn't think it was.

"It would mean a lot to Julia. She still loves him." I stopped. "I don't know. I don't know if it's a good idea. All I can do is put myself in Mami's place. If I loved someone . . . and I was dying . . . I would want to see them." I had the feeling that both Alma and Noah knew I was thinking about Rosario just then.

"What if he says something to hurt her? The guy is a first-class A-hole," Alma protested.

"I'm going down with you," Noah said. "You need muscle."

All Alma could do was shake her head and mutter something about men as we walked by her.

Fernando was leaning on the hood of his running car, blowing on his gloveless hands. He ignored me and kept his eyes on Noah. "You the kid from the fish market!" Fernando exclaimed, proud of his memory. "You grew up." Noah glowered at him in response. Fernando quickly turned to me. "Where's the form?"

"Where's the check?" I responded. I noticed for the first time that both Noah and I were in T-shirts. I hugged myself to keep the cold out, but Noah's arms hung by his sides as loosely and effortlessly as if he were sunning himself on a Caribbean island.

Fernando dug into the inside of his coat and handed me a check. "Public Bank? Is that a real bank?" Then I looked at the amount. "Three thousand? You kidding!" Noah took a step toward Fernando.

"It's what we can come up with in a hurry. Sunny borrowed the money from an uncle."

I turned to Noah. "Let's go back inside. We came out for nothing."

Fernando held me by the arm. "Come on, man! Gimme a break! I'm doing my best here!"

With one swift and powerful motion, Noah grabbed Fernando by the neck. "Tell me how hard to squeeze," Noah said.

I waited until Fernando's face turned pink and then nodded to Noah to ease up on his grip. Fernando sputtered, stuck a finger in Noah's face. "You don't know who you messin' with, fish boy. You don't know what you done. I'll find you."

"You don't have to find me. I can tell you where I'll be." Noah pushed his chest against Fernando's.

I pulled Noah away. "Let's go back in. I'm freezing." I offered the check in my hand to Fernando. "Here," I said. "Tell Sunny to get an extra bed ready." I turned and started to walk away.

"What you want from me? It's all I can do!"

I stopped. Thought for a moment and then turned to face him. "I'll take the three thousand for now and you can sign the form on one condition."

"What?"

It was hard to believe that this was the man who once broke a dinner plate on my head. He seemed so small and powerless just then.

"The form is upstairs. You come up, sign the form, and say hello to Julia. Five minutes with her. Tell her you'll look out for Javier. You'd be lying to her but lying is all you've ever done."

"No way." But he was thinking about it. He could go back

and tell Sunny he had gotten them all out of the Javier mess for a measly three thousand dollars. The five minutes with Julia? There was no need for Sunny to know about that.

Noah whispered, loud enough for Fernando to hear: "Hey, what you doing? You let him sign that form and that check is all you ever going to see."

"Come on up before I change my mind," I said to Fernando.

"I'm not leaving my car out on the street."

I looked at the car and said, "Relax, no one's gonna bother that thing."

Fernando thought about it for a few more moments and then went over to turn the motor off. We went inside with me leading the way, Fernando in the middle, and Noah in the rear. Just before we went inside the apartment, I turned to Fernando and said: "You say anything hurtful to her, I will hunt you down and I will make you and your family pay."

He moved closer to me and when he spoke, drops of spittle hit my face. "You think I'm afraid of you? You and your fish market friend?" Here he turned and looked at Noah. "I met peoples lots tougher than you in the oven and dealt with them. I'm going along with this so's not to hear from either of you ever again. You people are like a hemorrhoid. Now let's get this show over with."

And that's what it was—a show. But it was worth it to see Julia's eyes fill with life and light when I told her that Fernando had come to see her. I don't know what Fernando said to Julia for the ten minutes he was with her. I studied his face when he came out, looking for signs of transformation, but there were none. He signed the consent form and took a picture of the document with his phone.

"You want to see your son?" I asked. Javier had come out of his room and was standing in the hallway looking at us.

Fernando followed my eyes and for a second I thought I saw something like fatherly pride in his expression. Javier stood there, quietly defiant, not only not asking anything from his father but ready to refuse anything offered.

"No." Fernando was both answering my question and conveying a message to Javier. The last thing Fernando did was spit at Noah's feet.

After Fernando left, I gave the check to Noah so he could cash it for me. I went in to see Julia. She opened her eyes when I held her hand. "Gracias," she said softly.

"Was he nice to you?"

"He tried." Julia smiled. She had seen behind the charade I orchestrated but was grateful nonetheless. "He told me all about his job at Costco. I always knew he had a good head on his shoulders." She closed her eyes and mumbled, "Deep down he still loves me." I smiled, but maybe my smile was not convincing, because Julia said, "You got your Rosario. I got my Fernando."

We looked at each other for a long time with a kind of knowing, loving sadness. We understood each other. Mother and son.

Monday, March 6

When I stepped out of Julia's room this afternoon, Roberta asked if she could talk to me in private. We walked into my room. She closed the door and said, embarrassed, "I just got a call from my boss. Your mother's health insurance is refusing to pay for hospice. My boss has been on the phone with them and they're not budging."

"What?" I felt my knees buckle. I held on to the back of the chair.

"You could take her to a charity hospice. We're for profit. I'm very sorry."

"I can pay you. What do you charge?" I thought of the three thousand dollars that Noah had cashed for me.

Roberta shook her head sadly. "My boss is pulling me out. We only work where there is health insurance or . . ."

"Rich people." I filled in her sentence.

"I'm very sorry. I can only stay here until my shift ends at four. In about an hour." Her tone was businesslike, her expression hard as stone.

"I don't understand. If I left my mother at the hospital her health insurance would pay for that. But if I bring her home, they won't?"

"It's different."

"Didn't anyone check her health insurance before she left the hospital?"

"Yes, of course, I wouldn't be here if we hadn't. There was a misunderstanding about the coverage. My supervisor said someone in upper management at the insurance company reversed the initial decision."

"A misunderstanding?" I could feel my cheeks get hot. "A misunderstanding? That's my mother in that room!" Roberta showed no fear, not even the slightest reaction to my raised voice. This was not the first misunderstanding about payment for the care of the dying she had encountered. I took a deep breath. "I can give you three thousand dollars today. How much time with you will that get me?"

Roberta smiled a sad little smile. It was the first time she'd expressed any kind of emotion. "I might be able to stay until the end of Wednesday. I have some days off. End of Wednesday. That's all. My fee is five hundred dollars for a twelve-hour shift."

"Okay. And after Wednesday?"

After a long pause, Roberta answered. "You may be able to stretch your money with the right combination of less expensive care attendants. Have NPs come when restricted medications need to be administered and less expensive care-givers for the rest. You need people who can work the lung aspirator, the IV, give medications for when your mother's pain becomes unbearable."

"NPs?"

"Nurse practitioners. I can give you names of NPs who do independent work. I'm going to check on your mother."

I pulled out my desk chair and dropped myself onto it. I put my elbows on my desk and grabbed my head. I kept repeating Roberta's words, spoken so matter-of-factly: *when your mother's pain becomes unbearable.*

Tuesday, March 7

Last night, I don't know what time it was, I woke up to Mami's cries. When I entered her room, I turned on the lamp beside her bed and saw she was asleep. A nightmare. I held her hand. I put her oxygen mask back on. I whispered to her that I was there, that she was not alone, but wherever she was, it was beyond the reach of my words. I got the impression that the enemy she was facing required all her concentration and strength. I pulled up a chair and sat next to her. I remembered one time Mami telling me a joke she heard. Two men were in a plane that was going down fast and about to crash.

"Do you know any prayers?" one asks.

"No," says the other, "but I used to live next to a Catholic church and could hear them pray: B-17, O-25, N-34."

Mami laughed and laughed when she told me that. So that's what I did. I started reciting bingo numbers and after a while she calmed down. I fell asleep sitting next to her, and when I woke up morning light was streaming through the window and Javier was standing next to me.

"Is she dead?" he asked, a note of fear in his voice.

I stood quickly and put my hand on Julia's chest. It was moving. "She's still with us," I said, relieved.

"It stinks in here," Javier said, wrinkling his nose.

I opened the window to let fresh, cold air into the room. I walked over to the bag that contained all the items that Mrs. Santini had been instructed to buy. There was a box of latex gloves, cleansing wipes, adult diapers, and a package of something called slide sheets. On the slide sheets package there was a picture of a man being rolled on his side by a nurse while a second nurse tucked the sheet under him. Javier was standing next to Julia, a shocked, disbelieving look on his face. Was the stinking body in front of him the same person who raised him? "I need you to help me change her diaper," I said to him.

"No way," he said, terrified.

251

"Be a man," I said, grabbing him by the shoulders and waiting for him to look at me. "She's our mother."

"Okay," he finally said.

"You just have to hold her while I clean her." I turned off the oxygen and lifted Mami on her side and waited for Javier. He reached over across the bed and grabbed her shoulders. Now and then, when I was cleaning her, I would look at Javier. His eyes were everywhere except on Julia, as if seeing our mother's fragile body hurt him more than he expected. When I was done cleaning Julia, Javier walked quietly out of the room. I had the feeling he was about to cry.

I was lifting Julia's head to put a clean pillow under her when she opened her eyes. "I'm sorry," she whispered.

"Hey, how you feeling'?"

She ignored my question and asked, "Javier?"

"He was here. He went to get you some water," I lied. "He'll be back in a minute. We're all okay. Are you in pain?"

"It hurts. All over. Even my feet. Why my feet?" She tried to laugh, but only managed to cough a few times. "Thank you for bringing me home." She turned her head sideways toward the window. It was still open. I moved to close it, but she touched my arm. "Leave it open a little longer."

"Are you hungry? Mrs. Santini made you some soup. The kind you like with the little meatballs."

She shook her head. "There's something very nasty inside my head." Julia touched the side of her head and moaned. "Like . . . it's eating my brains. It burns . . . it hurts to think. I can't stop it. All I can do is let it eat."

"I can get you a cold towel."

She grabbed my hand and squeezed. I wished at that moment that she could transmit to me all the pain she was feeling. "I'm not afraid," she said, grimacing. "It hurts more than I imagine, but I'm not afraid. I'm only . . . afraid for you and Javier. That's the real, real dolor. It hurts so much. Leaving you two."

"We're going to be okay."

"Javier is not bad. He's good, deep down. You know that, right?"

"Like Fernando." The words came out of my mouth without thinking.

She licked her lips and waited for a spasm of pain to lessen. "No, not like Fernando. Like you. You the only one he got."

I dabbed the tears coming out of her eyes with my index finger. I wanted to give her something hopeful. I knew what hurt her the most was Javier's future. I said the only hopeful thing I could think of: "Someone told me about a school that would be good for him. In upstate New York. Near Elmira. I'm going to get him there. I promise."

Julia looked at me with eyes that said *this is not a time for lies*. It hurt me to have her look at me that way. Something tore inside and my eyes filled with tears. I stepped away. I grabbed a tissue from the night table, blew my nose, and when I stood in front of her again, she looked as if she was afraid to ask me something. "Nico . . ." she gasped.

"Rest now." I tried to put the oxygen mask on her face, but she waved it away.

"Let me tell you something. I need to."

"Okay."

"When I got pregnant and then you were born, I thought, now this baby means I'm stuck with this man I don't love. For a little while I didn't want you. That's the truth. I hated my life. Then I said, well, here's this baby now and he's mine to take care. He needs me. Then little by little it happened that the hate left me and the baby, you, that baby was you, you gave me life again." Julia closed her eyes and when she opened them again, she reached out and held on to my hand. "You don't see it now, but Javier can be like you were for me. He'll give you what you gave me." Julia took my hand to her lips and kissed it softly. Then she closed her eyes again. I started to go out when I heard her say, "Nico, let me talk to Javier for a second."

Javier was sitting on the living room sofa holding a glass of water. He looked shocked. It was as if death, the thing the X-Tecas talked about so lightly, had suddenly become real for him. "Hey," I said, shaking him. "Mami's awake now. She wants to see you."

Javier didn't move. I grabbed him by the shoulders, stood him up, and pointed him in the direction of the hallway. "She's not going to be around much longer. Go on now. She's waiting for you." I gave him a slight push and he turned around and glared at me. "Don't be a coward. She's only dying." He stared at me for a few more seconds and then walked slowly, hesitantly toward our mother's room.

Yeah, Nico. Don't be a coward.

There was a plastic bag with garbage by the door. I went out the hallway and threw it down the garbage chute. On my way back I stopped by Alma's door. The TV was on. Cartoons. I made a fist and raised my hand to knock on the door, but I stopped myself. I was looking for Rosario. She could make Javier laugh like no one else. Julia and Javier. I had forgotten their friendship. They played checkers together. Rosario would help him with school projects. How was it I was never jealous of Javier? The ease that Rosario had when she was with him. With me there was always a distance , a speck of caution that I didn't get too close. Also, I remembered the sadness that filled Javier after Rosario died. I was so engrossed in my own loss I didn't see Javier's. What did I want to say to Rosario? Can you come and make Javier a little kid again? I didn't knock.

Javier was grabbing his jacket from the closet when I went into our apartment. "Where you going?" He shrugged. "Did you talk to Mami?"

"She wanted me to go to some school. Said you'd take me there. She said it was her last wish and made me promise. What school?"

The school in Elmira. Joseph Delgado's hope for Javier. The same hope I grabbed on to out of nowhere and passed on to Julia. I said it only to make her feel good. But she believed me. Now Julia was holding me to my words. "You promised? What exactly did you promise?"

Javier gulped. "I said I'd go see it. That's all. She wouldn't let me go till I said it."

"But did you promise? Did you say the words *I promise?*"

Javier studied me. He looked scared. "Yeah, why?"

"Listen," I said, "a promise to a dying person is something very serious. Go ahead, ask your X-Teca homies if that isn't true." I could almost see what was happening inside Javier's head. Was I pulling one over on him? I myself did not know whether I was deadly serious or just trying to trick him. I only knew that I too had made a promise to Julia so whatever I said to Javier applied to me as well. I too had used those words when I told Julia I'd get Javier to the school in Elmira. *I promise.* What do they mean, really, those two words? Either they mean something precious and true, or they are just words.

Javier's face turned a shade paler. When he spoke again, there was no trace of the X-Teca bravado he usually carried around. "She grabbed my arm real hard. Wouldn't let go until I said the words."

I nodded. "Well, all right. What matters now is that you said them to your dying mother. It's done."

"What's done? What happens now? Anyways you aint' got the cash for no school." Javier's voice was shaky. At that moment, he was my little brother again.

"It's a promise that needs to be honored. That's all."

I was talking to myself as well as to Javier.

257

Wednesday, March 8

Another day. It started with Alma letting in a man with two jumbo-size oxygen tanks in a dolly. Roberta led the man to my mother's room. It was Roberta's last day with us. I had one of the NPs from her list lined up for tomorrow. Noah and Mrs. Santini had gone out to buy medical supplies from a list that Roberta gave them. Alma offered me a cookie and a cup of instant coffee, the only kind we had in the house. We sat at the kitchen table.

"You okay?" Alma asked.

"I need to see Primo."

"Javier?"

I shook my head. "Money. I need an advance on some

business Primo proposed. My mother's health insurance won't cover hospice care at home. Roberta informed me the other day. Yesterday or . . . the day before. I'm losing track."

"Some business Primo proposed? That doesn't sound good. I have a little money."

"You don't have the kind of money we need. I looked in your globe the other day and borrowed one hundred."

"I know."

"Sorry. I should've told you."

Alma brushed my apology away with a flick of her hand and said, "I might be able to get some money from Ruben."

"Why is Ruben's money good enough but not Primo's? It's the same source." I stopped. Both Alma and Rosario had this expression that never failed to melt my heart. It came over them whenever I said or started to say something hurtful. It was a look full of compassion, like they understood the real reason behind my words. "I'm just . . . worried."

"How's Sabrina?" Alma asked casually as she blew on her coffee.

I began to cough and choke. I looked and saw my phone on the table. "You read my texts?" I sounded more indignant than I was.

"Of course. Why wouldn't I?"

"Maybe because a man needs a little privacy? How you open my phone? You know my password?"

"Like that was hard to crack. 121805 Rosario's birthday. What's all this about a novel you wrote?"

"Save the inquisition for another day. It's a long story and today is not a good day for long stories." I bit half a cookie and began to chew. The last thing I needed just then was questions about my literary theft. Fortunately, Alma seemed more interested in other information discovered in my texts.

"What are you doing, exactly, with Sabrina?"

I finished chewing and then washed down the crumbs in my mouth with coffee. There was always a place in my conversations with Alma when the jesting and ribbing turned serious, and we had just entered that space. "I don't exactly know what I'm doing," I admitted. "Trying to forget what's happening in my life, feeling sorry for my miserable self."

"At the expense of some poor girl's feelings?" When I didn't answer, Alma said bitterly, "You're lying to her, aren't you? Why doesn't that surprise me?"

"I have never lied to her . . . about how I feel about her. She was . . . something exciting. Is that so bad? Alma, come on. Don't be so hard on me. You accept other people's flaws, no problem. Ruben's, for example; why not mine? Why don't you ever give me a break?"

Roberta came out and stood there waiting to be recognized. "I'm leaving at three. Your mother will be okay the rest of the day and tonight. I need to take the restricted pain medication with me when I leave, but I'll leave you some pills you can give her if needed. I'll drop by tomorrow and give the restricted medication to a licensed practitioner."

"I got someone. Tasha Brown. From your list."

Roberta wrinkled her nose. "She'll have to do." She turned around without waiting for a response and went back to my mother's room.

"She's a little scary, isn't she?" Alma asked when we heard the door to my mother's room close. I took Alma's gentle tone as a sign that we should move on from the previous conversation.

"I'm so tired," I said. Then, out of nowhere: "You never told me about Rosario's laptop."

Alma shook her head, but not angrily. More like a *here we go again* shake. "What about it?"

"She killed it by running water over it. I went to the Stardust. Talked to the manager or owner."

"You go to the Stardust. You lie to girls. You make deals with Primo." She folded her arms as if to comfort herself from what she was about to say. "You remind me of her. Those few days before . . . like she already knew she was going to die. She was both unhinged and resigned all at once."

Unhinged and resigned. I had to smile at Alma's precise diagnosis. I shut my eyes and squeezed the back of my neck as if to keep a painful memory from reaching my head. "If she killed her laptop . . ."

"Chances are she took her own life on purpose. Okay?" Alma stopped and then said, "It doesn't mean you have to do the same."

Alma picked up cookie crumbs from the table and dropped them into her cup. I could tell that beneath her sad expression, she was trying to decide whether to tell me something that would most probably hurt both me and her. When I looked into her eyes, I felt as if my head were a fishbowl and my feelings for Rosario a lonely, very visible, goldfish. "I didn't tell you about Rosario's laptop because . . . I don't know. Part of it was respecting Rosario's privacy. Part of it was . . . I know how much . . . she meant to you. It seemed hurtful to tell you. I didn't want to destroy . . ."

"The Rosario I remember," I finished her sentence.

Alma grinned as if to let me know she understood more than I could possible ever know. After a while, she said, "You have people counting on you. Julia. Javier." She paused and I thought she was going to say "me," but she didn't. She pushed herself away from the table and stood up. She took her cup to the sink and began to wash it. With her back to me, she said, "You have friends who support you. Rosario had people counting on her also. She had me and Pepito just like you have Julia and Javier. She had friends supporting her. She even had people who . . . loved her." Alma looked at me and I could see the sadness in her. Then she continued softly, "But she turned all that down, responsibilities, support, love. She made a choice. Do you understand?"

What I thought about just then was the dream about Joseph and the Pharaoh that Ruth told me about what seemed like ages ago. The dream predicted famine but Joseph changed the outcome of the dream. Rosario had chosen death, but I could choose life. I could change the outcome of my dream. That was what Ruth and Alma were telling me.

I went over to Alma and kissed the top of her head. "I hate you. You know that, right?"

"Me too you," she answered, barely audible.

Thursday, March 9

At 6:00 a.m, I was splashing cold water on my face when my cell phone rang.

"This is Tasha Brown. The RN you hired for this morning?"

"Yes?" I said, dreading what she would say.

"I'm sorry. I can't make it today. I got a sick child."

"What? What do you mean? Do you know anyone else who can come?"

"No, your best bet is to call 911. Get your mother back in the hospital. So sorry. I gotta go."

I found and tapped Roberta's number.

"This is Nico, from yesterday. The RN I got to come at nine

just canceled. Can you please come with her medications? Give them to her this morning. I'll pay you."

There was the sound of a throat clearing phlegm. Then: "I can be there at nine. But I can't give her medications. You need to have someone whot's licensed to sign for them by then."

"Please! I gave her the pills, but she's still in pain. I don't know if I can find anyone by nine."

"I can hand over the medications to someone who's certified. That's all I can do. Neither me nor Calvary Care can treat your mother anymore. I'll be there around nine. If there's no one qualified there, I'll have to return the meds to the hospital. That's the best I can do."

When Roberta hung up, I left a message with Dr. Zimmerman and waited for him to call me back. I went back to Julia's room and sat by her bed. I watched her arch her back as if there were hot coals underneath her. I saw her bite her hand to keep herself from screaming. After an hour or so, she finally went to sleep. Still no call from Dr. Zimmerman. Then I remembered Ruth telling me that her parents owned the urgent care on Southern Boulevard. Her father was a physician, and her mother was a nurse. I was embarrassed to call. Not only did I steal her manuscript, but there I was begging for medical help.

"I'm in a bind," I said straight out when she answered. "My mother is dying with all kinds of cancer. She's hurting bad. The hospice service refuses to treat her because her health insurance doesn't cover hospice. They're bringing her medications at nine, but they'll only hand them over to someone licensed."

"Hold on." I could hear Ruth speaking to someone but could not make out what she was saying. "My dad wants to know the name of your mom's oncologist, the one prescribing the medications."

"Dr. Zimmerman at BronxCare."

"What's your address?" I gave her my address. Then: "We'll be there in twenty minutes."

I looked at my phone. It was 8:15. My mother had opened her eyes again. I grabbed her hand and kissed it. "I think you're going to be okay, Mami. We're going to make you comfortable. Is there anything you want? Anyone you want me to get? A priest?"

Julia waved her hand. She whispered: "No. Too many sins. Poor guy." She winked at me. "Doña Hortensia."

"You got it," I said.

She motioned for me to come closer. She spoke with difficulty, a raspy breath that smelled of rotten apples. She was

266

having trouble swallowing so I had her drink a sip of water from a plastic cup with a straw. She nodded for me to take it away and said: "Tell Harrison . . . to sue Lux Linen. Eleven years. No masks, nothing." Julia grimaced. I put the oxygen mask back on her and smoothed her hair.

Dr. Silvester got ahold of Dr. Zimmerman and they agreed for Dr. Silvester to be the prescribing physician during Julia's hospice. When Roberta showed up, Mrs. Silvester, a soft-spoken woman with white hair tied in a ponytail took the bag of medications from Roberta, signed for them, and told Roberta, in a very nice way, that she was going to report Calvary Care to the Department of Health.

Dr. Silvester and his wife disappeared into my mother's room. Ruth and I sat at the kitchen table drinking instant coffee. I felt overwhelmed with guilt. The guilt was like a cinder block tied to my tongue. I had trouble speaking. How could I tell Ruth that I had claimed her novel as my own?

"So, going to Cornell in the fall still in the works?"

"Yes. It's all settled. I just got my dorm assignment."

"Is Ithaca close to Elmira?" I asked. It was either that or confess my thievery.

"I think so. Why?"

"There's a school for at-risk kids there. I promised my

267

mother I would take my little brother, Javier." I was surprised that I had used the word *promise*. But yeah, I had done that. I had made a promise.

"Oh. Elmira's a short drive from Cornell. If Javier goes there, you can come by and visit. The fall is beautiful up north." Ruth turned bright red. I smiled. I thought about my dream. If I were to carry out my promise to Julia, I'd have to take Javier to the school in Elmira before my death in the summer. I had the feeling Ruth remembered my dream as well just then. I saw her take a deep breath, as if gathering courage to speak something that was difficult to say: "You still think your dream will come true?"

"The part in the dream where my mother is not there is coming true," I said, remembering one of the empty chairs.

"But you can still change the outcome of the rest of the dream," Ruth said quickly.

"Like Joseph," I said, smiling.

"Yes. Maybe your dream was like that, a good dream after all. Maybe your dream is showing you a path to take more than a prediction."

"A path? What path?"

"Your writing. Your journal. You still doing it?"

I wasn't sure whether Ruth was answering my question or changing the subject. "Yes . . . for some reason."

"It's who you are," she said quickly, spontaneously. Then, embarrassed, "I mean, it must be what you're meant to be doing."

I felt, suddenly, something like an explosion inside me. The words I was writing seemed so poor and so ordinary in comparison to Rosario's or Ruth's, but they were me, they were true, they were the kind of words I was meant to be writing. I was proud of myself, for the effort, such as it was.

Ruth lowered her eyes, as she had in my dream, as if to let me have a quiet space to feel what I was feeling. After a while, I thought of confessing what I'd done with her work to Ruth, but it didn't seem like the right moment. So we waited, in a comfortable silence, until we heard the door to my mother's room open, and Ruth and I pushed our chairs back and stood up at the same time. We walked to the living room to meet Dr. Silvester. "Can you help your mother?" he said to Ruth. Ruth walked down the hall to Julia's room. Dr. Silvester pointed to the sofa and I sat down. He sat in the easy chair in front of me.

"Your mother will soon enter what we call in hospice the

transition phase. She's not there yet. In the transition phase, she will be mostly unconscious. Not totally. Even when you think she's unconscious, she will hear you. Her pain will be controlled from now on. Either myself or my wife or one of our staff will come by and give her the medications she needs. We'll make sure her lungs are clear."

"Thank you. I have some money," I said, embarrassed.

"I will accept whatever you can give me. Later. It will be used to help others." There was a pause during which I thought he was waiting for me to ask a question, but the only question I could think of was *why?* Why was my mother dying?

Dr. Silvester reached over and patted my knee. "You are now the primary caregiver for your mother. You must arrange for others to help you. Emma and I will handle her medical needs, you don't have to worry about that. But the rest is up to you. Do you have other friends who can be with her while you take a break? It's important that you care for yourself and your brother. Ruth said you had a brother."

"Yes, I can take it from here. Thank you."

"Now go see your mother. Emma will show you how to keep her comfortable."

Mrs. Silvester was both efficient and gentle. Her thin,

strong hands could move my mother without any sign of discomfort or pain appearing on my mother's face. The most amazing thing was how Julia's face brightened when Ruth was by her side. "You're the angel I was waiting for," Julia said to Ruth.

Then she turned to me and gave me a meaningful look.

Friday, March 10

At some point during the night, I stretched out on the floor next to Julia and fell instantly asleep. When I woke up, light was streaming through the window, Julia was sleeping peacefully, and Alma was sitting in the chair next to the hospital bed. I stood and motioned for Alma to follow me. "I can't believe I fell asleep," I said, when we were out.

"You look worn out. Why don't you go rest? Ruth's mom called. She's on her way over."

We were standing in front of the fridge. I opened it and took out the package of eggs and the chorizo I had bought earlier. "Want some breakfast?" When I turned around, I saw that Alma was holding my phone. "You gotta be kidding me. You reading my messages again?" I snatched my phone out of her hand.

"I was bored. I didn't bring my phone. People have been calling. Noah's coming over around eleven. I called Ruben. He said Javier went somewhere with Primo."

I placed the eggs and the chorizo back in the fridge. Making eggs and chorizo seemed like a task more complicated than I could handle now. Alma grabbed me by the shoulders and sat me down. "I'll make the eggs. Sit down. You always make them too runny anyway." Alma took out a plastic bowl from one of the cabinets and began to crack the eggs over it. "Mixing the eggs in a bowl with a little milk rather than cracking them directly over the pan is an Anglo thing, but it works better." When all the eggs were in the bowl, she cut the chorizo into small pieces and put them in a pan over the stove. Immediately the room filled with a delicious smell. Alma continued talking as she did all this. "Ruth and me worked out a schedule for people to be with your mom. Two-hour shifts during the day and four-hour shifts during the night. Is Harrison still in the picture? We could use him."

"I think he's pulling away. Too much for him."

"He's a wimp. I could have told you that."

I remembered asking Harrison about guardianship papers for Javier when I was gone. But if my dream was true, Javier would be dead before me. There were two empty chairs in that funeral parlor. Why did it bother me now that the dream predicted Javier's death? Could be the kid just refused to show up to my funeral. No, Alma and Noah would get him there somehow. Alma had been speaking for a minute and I had not heard a word she said. "What?"

"I was just asking if you planned to see Sabrina on Sunday." Here she turned her head around and gave the kind of look that would scare anyone not used to receiving it. I grabbed my phone and read the text from Sabrina, the same text that Alma had already read.

> Hi—do you still want to see me? Mom invited
> Laura Benson to join us for dessert. I didn't
> know she did that. Laura read some of your
> novel (Mom sent it to her—sorry!) and Laura's
> super excited to meet you. Dad also. It won't
> be all serious. It'll be fun. If you're interested.
>
> See you.

Alma began to warm a flour tortilla over one of the gas burners. *"It'll be fun,"* she said with a fake, falsetto voice.

"Please don't," I said, trying not to smile.

"What novel?" Alma took out a plate and then put a tortilla filled with egg and chorizo on top of it.

I swallowed and then mumbled: "Ruth's novel. I somehow let Sabrina believe I wrote it." Saying it out loud was so much worse than thinking it. Alma stood there, a look of disbelief on her face.

"I . . . I don't even know what to say." She lowered herself onto a chair. "I mean, can you sink any lower?"

"Probably." I pushed the plate with the egg and chorizo tortilla away from me. I stood and was about to go to my room when I stopped and asked, "Who was Rosario seeing? There was a guy with her at the Stardust. Earlier that evening. Her dealer? Who was giving her the smack?" I asked. I sounded irritated. I was irritated at myself more than anything.

"Ah, Rosario again," Alma sighed. "I don't know. I have no idea who she saw that day or who was supplying her. What would you do if you found out?"

"Probably kill him." I meant for it to be humorous, or slightly humorous, but it didn't come out that way.

"Nico, listen to you. Can you see what she's doing to you?"

"What she's doing to me?" It had never occurred to me that Rosario was *doing* something to me. But she was, wasn't she? "I guess she's making me resigned and whatever." I said it with kindness. I knew Alma was worried about me.

"Unhinged and resigned."

"So . . . I mean . . . what can I do?" I didn't know. I honestly didn't know.

"Don't be like Rosario. Don't go at it as if you had no people to care for or caring for you. Talk to Noah or Ruth or even me. Just speak about what's hurting you."

I managed a sad kind of smile and said: "I think I hear Julia. Thank you, Almita."

On Alma's face—the look of love offered, but not returned.

Saturday, March 11

Aconversation with Noah in our living room while Julia slept.

"Hey, is there something you wanna say to me? Now's the time. Go ahead . . . be a man and say it."

"You're drunk. I thought you were going to stop after you left the hospital."

"I will stop. I'm drinkin' to keep you company. Tonight's the last time. Come on . . . drunks tell the truth."

"Did Alma put you up to this?"

"Okay . . . listen to me . . . I'll go first. Show you how it's done."

"Go ahead."

"Go head what?"

"You were gonna go first about something."

"Yeah, yeah. Okay, here it goes: She never really loved me . . . you already knew that . . . don't lie. No lying."

"She loved you."

"Yeah . . . not like . . . true love. She cared for me. I was like . . . something to hold her steady when she started to go adrift . . . But I wasn't enough, ya know. Truth is—I always knew I wasn't the real thing . . . true love, ya know?"

"You were good. Good for her."

"Not good enough. Okay . . . your turn. What's on your mind."

"You already know. You've always known."

"Say it! Say the words!"

"I loved her."

"Nah, that's not it. Try again, damn it!"

"I love her."

"Better. What else?"

"I thought . . . she . . . maybe loved me."

"Maybe she did, bro. Could be she did."

Silence.

Sunday, March 12

I drove down the Hutchinson River Parkway at forty miles an hour with angry commuters honking, flashing their lights behind me, and shouting obscenities when they were finally able to pass me. I was driving slowly to better let the thoughts inside me play themselves out. What the hell was I doing? Going to talk to an editor about a book I didn't write while my mother was back home dying. The closer I got to the Scarsdale exit, the worse I felt about myself, and yet, I couldn't make myself turn around.

When I finally found the red-brick and white-trim mansion, I slowed down and then stopped a few feet from the entrance to their driveway. Light, fluffy snow was falling and the whole house, with the warm lights emanating from it, seemed like the scene in a snow globe. It was a place that was incredibly attractive and incredibly foreign. I imagined myself living there, no X-Tecas, no lugging fish crates, no Javier, no urine smell on the stairs, and knew at once that it would be both wonderful and so not . . . me.

I started the truck and was about to enter Sabrina's driveway when my phone buzzed.

"Hey, where are you?" Noah sounded angry.

"In Scarsdale."

"Seriously? Scarsdale? Right now? You need to get your ass back here."

"Mami . . ."

"She's fading fast. Organ failure, Mrs. Silvester says. Could be soon."

"Is Javier there?"

"No. Alma and Ruben are heading over to the park to get him. Get down here!"

Mommy was unconscious by the time I got back from Scarsdale. The apartment was full of people. Javier was sitting on the living room sofa in between Noah and Sal. On Javier's face I could see something like terror. Sal had an unlit cigar in his mouth and I could tell he was itching to light it. Mrs. Santini, Ruth, Alma, and her mother sat around the kitchen table. I looked around the room at people's faces and thought that I had arrived too late. But then I saw Alma shake her head. As usual, she had read my mind. Mrs. Santini stood and came toward me with open arms. She hugged me and said, "Thank God you're back. Doña Hortensia is with her now. Alma thought your mother would want her rather than Father Alonso." Mrs. Santini glanced at Alma with a look of disapproval. "Mrs. Silvester is there also. I didn't want Doña Hortensia to be in there alone with your mom. I'll let them know you're here."

I gestured at Javier to come with me. When he didn't move, Sal and Noah pushed him off the sofa. We stood by the doorway. The door to Mami's bedroom opened and Doña Hortensia came out. She leaned closer to me and whispered, "Your mother will feel your presence and your love even if she doesn't show it. If you speak to her, she'll hear you." Then she peered deeply into Javier's eyes, as if warning him to leave his canicas of hate outside the room.

The room was dark. The only light was from the night-stand lamp, which had been covered with one of Mami's dark blouses. Mrs. Silvester motioned for us to come over and sit on two chairs next to her bed. The bed had been lowered so that, as we sat, Mami's face was slightly below us. Mami was gripping a rosary I had never seen before. An agitated movement of her hands rattled the beads of the rosary. I could see her eyeballs move inside her eyelids. Whatever she was seeing, it was not peaceful. I looked at Mrs. Silvester and asked silently what was happening.

"She's not in pain," Mrs. Silvester answered. "She's letting go of the familiar and entering a new place. Her suffering has a happy ending."

"Can I touch her?"

"Of course," Mrs. Silvester said. "But you don't have to. She knows you're here."

Mrs. Silvester left the room. I glanced at Javier. His jaw and fists were clenched as if to keep impending sobs from surfacing. I almost expected him to bolt out of the chair and out of the apartment at any moment. "You want to say something to her?"

Javier shook his head.

I held on to her hand and after a while I spoke. I'm not sure if I was speaking to Javier or to Mami. "Thank you for the Christmases. That green plastic tree that you keep in the closet and that you make us decorate every year. The box with the stable and the clay Jesus and animals you take out.

282

I'm sorry about the donkey I dropped. Thank you for the tamales you make. For the sweater you knitted me. Thank you for working all those years at Lux Linen. Thank you for taking care of us." I elbowed Javier and whispered: "Say something." I elbowed him.

"Thanks for the Xbox," he finally said.

I could barely hear his words, they were spoken so softly, but just then I felt like a big brother to him. I remembered playing Nerf basketball in my room with him when he was four and I was nine. I remember going to his room when he had nightmares and lying next to him until he fell asleep. I thought of asking him to speak louder, but I realized that it wasn't necessary. Julia heard him. Javier stayed with me for another ten minutes and then he got up and left. I didn't go after him.

Monday, March 13

Julia died this morning at 4:12 a.m. In the last hours of her life, she entered a good place. Her breathing slowed down and I even saw a smile appear momentarily on her face now and then. I was holding her hand and watching her lips when the final breath eased gently out of her lips.

Tuesday, March 14

Julia Lozano—Her Life

1986—Born August 10, Monterrey, Mexico.

2002—Comes to the US when she's 16 years old.

2004—Marries Emir Kardos.

2006—Gives birth to Nicolás Kardos.

2008—Divorces Emir Kardos.

2009—Moves in with Fernando Rojas, the love of her life.

2011—Gives birth to Javier Rojas.

2012—Starts working at Lux Linen.

2013—Moves to Hunts Point Rehabs with Fernando. Nico is 7 and Javier is 2 years old.

2018—Fernando Rojas moves out.

2023—Dies March 13, 37 years old.

Friday, March 17

Things I remember about Julia's memorial service.

-Mr. Ortiz's funeral parlor. Exactly as in my dream.

-My mother's urn in the front. A picture of Julia sitting in front of a fake mountain scene. She's holding baby Javier on her knee. I'm next to her with a red cowboy hat.

-Javier trying unsuccessfully not to cry.

-My own tears gushing out when I saw the room full of

people. Lux Linen workers standing in the back. A nurse from BronxCare. People I've never seen before.

-My eulogy. That Julia liked people. Enjoyed talking to them. She believed people were good. Deep down. She worked hard for her two sons. We were her joy.

-Benny winking at me when I finished speaking.

-My father shaking my hand and putting a five-thousand-dollar check in my shirt pocket.

-Harrison telling me the judge approved guardianship in the nick of time. He put documents in the mail, including forms, in case something happens to me.

-Ruth hugging me.

Saturday, March 18

Julia, Mami. What was your life? Ordinary. Who knew about you? A few people. Work. Sacrifice. Love where you could find it. Pain. Your joy was your sons. Javier and Nico. You were not a nobody. You were somebody. I miss you so much, Mami. It hurts like everything not to make you laugh. It hurts. Mami. Open your eyes, you'd say, and see love in front of you. I don't know if I ever really saw you. There. Living a life that would end someday. Why you leave us? Javier and Nico. How you expect us to go on?

I don't want your life to be for nothing.

All you did, all you lived was for Javier and me. It can't that your sacrifice was a waste. I won't let it be.

What did I ever give you? I gave you life once, you told me. What can I give you now? Javier. Javier's life. That's a tough order, jefita. My own . . . to keep on living. Oof. But yeah. Okay. Let me see if there's a way.

I'm remembering now the way you looked at me when I told you about that school in Elmira, where I promised to take Javier. *This is not a time for lies*, you said to me without words. Okay, let me see what I can do. No lies. Let's see if I can be honest. There's some truths I have to face up to first. But, yes, I'll honor my promise. I won't let your life be for nothing.

Sunday, March 19

I made two calls yesterday. After I wrote the entry above. The first to Sabrina to tell her I had lied to her about *Orchidea*. She called me names, all true. When she asked why, all I could think was that I wanted to be somebody. I was a nobody and wanted to be somebody.

"I'm sorry."

I couldn't think of anything else to say.

The other call was to Joseph Delgado. He picked up on the first ring.

"This is Nico Kardos. Javier's brother. That school you mentioned. The one in Elmira."

"Yeah. Yeah. Good. You thought about it."

"What do I have to do?"

"You talking about taking him this summer?"

I remembered the second empty chair in my dream. "No. Sooner than that. As soon as I can get Javier there."

There was silence on the other end. Then, "Okay. It's doable. I know the person who runs it. It won't be a problem. They'll take Javier whenever you bring him."

"Assuming I can get him there, what's to say he'll stay and not run away?"

"Ah." I could hear Joseph breathing. He was thinking. "Listen, what if you stay a couple of weeks with him. You could help around the school or something. A week or two. Say to Javier that the school is something for both of you. Can you do that?"

"Me? . . . I don't know." I thought I might be able to save Javier, but I hadn't gone as far as saving myself. Both Javier and me living. Benny's words from way back then came to me. *Your mami—her fate is sealed. Your brother . . . well, there's still a wiggle of hope. It's up to him. Same goes for you. Nothing's set. You can choose.*

"Think about it. Both of you. With you there it could work. I know this place. After a couple of weeks, kids want to stay. I'll make some phone calls. It's a good decision, Nico."

292

I was about to hang up when I heard Joseph speak again. "Hey, before you go. I did some digging about the girl who overdosed, the one you wanted to know more about—the circumstances surrounding her death."

"Rosario." I could feel my heart speed up.

"You still interested?"

I hesitated. I was sitting on the floor of my bedroom. Leaning back on my bed. I stood. My legs buckled a little so I sat on the bed. "Go ahead."

"Lab report showed the dope was good-quality China white. It wasn't tainted. Also, there was no foul play. She went in with a guy around six p.m. He left a couple of hours later. We know she was alive and well when he left because she made a phone call to her teacher, Cortazar, around eleven. Time of death was around three a.m."

"Who?" I had trouble speaking. My mouth was dry. There was a pain in my stomach. "Who was the guy?"

"Couldn't make out his face. Someone with a limp. One of his shoes had a metal plate at the bottom. That's the only identifiable mark."

A shiver of recognition ran through me. "A what?"

"You know, a metal plate. Like they use for tap-dancing. Why? You know someone? It doesn't matter. She was alive after he left. That's why we didn't follow up on the guy. That's all we got. I'm going to go ahead and call my friend at Elmira right now. If you can stay a week or so, it would work. Javier will stay. I have a good feeling about this. Your brother can still be saved. I'll call you in a day or so, when I got everything lined up."

"Okay." I ended the call.

Primo accompanied Rosario to the hotel room and stayed with her for two hours. He supplied her with drugs. He was her supplier and lover. I tried to convince myself that Primo killed Rosario. Primo the cultivator of women and kids. Finding someone to hate was good. But in the end, hatred could not change the pain of knowing that Rosario chose to die, whether with cold purpose or impulsive recklessness.

What was it like for you, Rosario? The loneliness and darkness in that sordid hotel room, when you could not find a way out? I think I know.

Do I follow you?

Monday, March 20

A poem Rosario gave me for my sixteenth birthday.

For Nicolás
On his birthday
The Sidewalk Trees of Hunts Point
By Rosario Zamora
Those trees
Growing on square patches
Of hard dirt carved out of sidewalk
Skinny creatures breathing exhaust and exhaustion
Not awakening to whatever spring

Is Hunts Point's share

Already dying in early July

Could be you

Are the only one to love them

Tuesday, March 21

A week after Rosario broke up with Noah, a few days before her death, I went to Alma's apartment to print a homework assignment. I didn't think anyone was there, and then I heard sobbing coming from Rosario's room. She was on her bed crying. I sat on the edge of the bed. I asked if she was all right, if there was anything I could do.

"Just hug me," she said.

She turned away from me and I lay down next to her. I put my arms around her and she drew closer to me. At one point she said, "I don't like it here, Nicolas. I never will. I'm trying, but I can't."

I thought *here* was Hunts Point, Noah, Lushy Foods. It totally escaped me she might have been asking for help. I knew she had broken up with Noah a few days before and I asked if that's why she was sad.

"I love Noah," she said.

"But you broke up with him."

"I love him the way you love Alma."

"Is there someone else?"

She didn't answer me. I took her silence as a yes. She loved someone she didn't want to talk about. I smiled then, and I smile now as I write this. I asked her because I was expecting her to answer, *Yes, you.* I was convinced I was the person she secretly loved. She couldn't love me openly for the hurt that it would cause Alma. That's what I believed.

I stroked the back of her hair to comfort her. Something came over me just then and I told her I loved her, had always loved her, and would always love her. I told myself that when she turned around to face me and I began to kiss her tears, my words and kisses that followed were two people being honest with each other. She was telling me with her body what she could not say with words. We talked a little afterward. She told me I was different. She asked me if I thought she was a good writer. "Please, tell me the truth."

I told her, yes, she was a good writer. Now, thinking back, I don't think she believed me, just like I now know I wasn't the one she loved.

Wednesday, March 22

I walked into Javier's room a little while ago. He hasn't been home since Julia's memorial service. Hanging from one of his bedposts is a "box guitar" that we made together when he was in first grade. We took one of those plastic butter containers, cleaned it, and then wrapped five different-size rubber bands around it. Each rubber band made a different sound when plucked and I showed Javier how to play a song that Julia liked to sing.

Ay, ay, ay, ay
Canta y no llores

Porque cantando se alegran
Cielito lindo
Los corazones

For many years, sometimes at night, I would hear the twang of the rubber bands coming from Javier's room.

Cortazar was right about this journal—after doing it for a while I can see my ugly parts. Maybe so, but I also see some good things I had forgotten or didn't even know were there. Like the times when I was glad Javier was around. And when Javier saw this apartment as his whole world, his home. The family of three that we were would not have been the same without Julia, Javier and me.

I'm getting to the end of this journal. Maybe one or two more entries. Or this could be the last one depending on what happens tomorrow.

I've been emailing my teachers to tell them I'm going to be away for a while. Joseph has lined up a place for Javier at the Elmira School and I can stay there as well for as long as I want. My teachers all wrote back with things I can do so I can still graduate in May. What they require is doable if that's what I decide. I don't know. Right now, I'm so full of hate I don't see how I can continue living without killing Primo. But there's also love in there. For Javier—which is a surprise.

First, getting Javier out of Primo's grasp.

Okay, okay. I got nothing more to say.

Thursday, March 23

Rafito was guarding the entrance to the X-Tecas' house. I told him I was there to talk to Primo about business. Rafito led me to the second floor, where there were half a dozen X-Tecas lounging, drinking, playing video games. Javier was there, but I didn't speak to him. After a few minutes Primo came out of a back room.

"Nicolás. Good to see you. What up?" Primo pushed one of the X-Tecas out of a recliner and plopped himself down.

I stuck my hand in my left pocket and grasped the switchblade I'd found in Javier's room. I said, "I'm here for Javier." I took out the five thousand dollars I was carrying in my pocket. "This is so you let him walk out of here."

"Whoa!" Primo exclaimed. "I thought you were here on business—the one we talked about. What happened to the sales you were setting up for us?"

"This is business. That's what Javier is to you—business."

Primo studied Nico's face for a few minutes. "Hey, man, look, there's the kid. Take him. If he'll go with you."

I turned to Javier. "This is all the money we got. I'm giving it to Primo as a sign of respect. So he'll let us go and we can keep the promise we made to Mami. We go to that school she wanted you to go. We stay a couple of weeks. After that, if you want to come back, be an X-Teca, okay, I won't stand in your way."

Javier was silent, but I could tell that I had reached some deep part of him.

"Don't look like he's interested," Primo said, a smirk on his face. "Why don't you use that money to buy some product from me. Get yourself going on the business we talked about. We got plans for Javier."

I ignored Primo and kept my eyes on Javier. "He killed Rosario. He might as well have," I said, pointing with my chin in the direction of Primo. "He knew for sure she needed help and he took advantage of that. He used her. He uses people."

Javier looked at Primo. I saw in his eyes a flicker of anger. As if Javier was seeing a Primo he'd never seen before.

Primo laughed. "Ah, Rosario. She used to talk about you, you know. I asked her if you could ever be one of us. No, not Nicolás. You were gonna be a writer, like her. She was special. Rosario. Messed up, but special."

"You drew her to you. Got her addicted. Cultivated her."

"I never forced her. She wanted to get high. Just like she wanted me."

I stared at Primo. My rage, all my rage, became too powerful to contain. I found the button on Javier's switchblade. I saw in my mind's eye what would happen in the next few seconds. I would pop open the blade and stick it in Primo's heart. I saw it happen. My love for Rosario transformed to hate. Or both hate and love turned one. Then, just as the switchblade came out of my pocket, I felt a hand on my wrist, and when I turned, I saw Javier, holding me, giving me my life again.

"Let's go," he said. "Keep the cash. We gonna need it."

Acknowledgments

My writing vocation began when I was a sophomore at Jesuit High School in El Paso, Texas. That's when I started keeping a journal—a daily practice I continue to this day. I want to thank my teachers at Jesuit High, and in particular, John Hatcher S.J., who taught me the joy and responsibility of developing and using the gift of writing.

This novel started off in a different direction until my dear agent, Faye Bender, set it on its proper course. Emily Seife, my editor, found the truth in my story and brought it to light. Aurelia Kembel-Rodrigues, my young writer friend, helped me keep the voices of my characters authentic.

Finally, I want to thank Annie Dillard for her life's work. Her book *The Writing Life* has been a life-long inspiration and a reminder to write for the right reason.

About the Author

Francisco X. Stork (he/him) emigrated from Mexico at the age of nine with his mother and his adoptive father. He is the author of many novels, including *Marcelo in the Real World*, recipient of the Schneider Family Book Award; *The Memory of Light*, recipient of the Tomás Rivera Book Award; *Disappeared*, which received the Young Adult Award from the Texas Institute of Letters and was a Walter Dean Myers Award Honor Book; and *I am Not Alone*, which received three starred reviews. Visit him at franciscostork.com.